How to Be a Millionaire

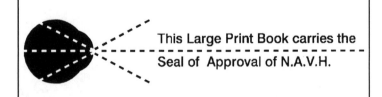

This Large Print Book carries the
Seal of Approval of N.A.V.H.

COLORADO CHRISTMAS: BOOK ONE

How to Be a Millionaire

Rosey Dow

THORNDIKE PRESS
A part of Gale, Cengage Learning

GALE
CENGAGE Learning™

Detroit • New York • San Francisco • New Haven, Conn • Waterville, Maine • London

LIBRARY OF CONGRESS CATALOGING-IN-PUBLICATION DATA

Dow, Rosey.
    How to be a millionaire : love comes in an unexpected
package during the 1880's / by Rosey Dow. — Large print ed.
        p. cm. — (Colorado Christmas ; bk. 1) (Thorndike Press
    large print Christian fiction)
    ISBN-13: 978-1-4104-3098-4
    ISBN-10: 1-4104-3098-7
    1. Miners—Fiction. 2. Bank fraud—Fiction. 3.
Colorado—History—1876–1950—Fiction. 4. Large type books. I.
Title.
PS3554.O89H69 2010
    813'.6—dc22   2010024167

Published in 2010 by arrangement with Barbour Publishing, Inc.

Printed in Mexico
1 2 3 4 5 6 7 14 13 12 11 10

To my daughter, Miriam Dow, who helps me with those pesky plot twists.

CHAPTER 1

Colorado Springs, Colorado, December 1890
At a small table near the kitchen door of their father's stylish restaurant, Penny Joshua leaned across the small table and said, "How much time will Mr. Campbell give you to find a backer for the mine?"

Worry in every line on his young face, her brother, Farley, replied, "The longest Campbell can give me is New Year's Day. After that, he'll have to start looking elsewhere. Otherwise, he won't make his production deadline in April. He has to get the equipment up here and hire a crew." He flung his hand down in an impatient gesture. "I'm going to be twenty-five years old in three more months. It's time I married Diane and got a start in life. Who knows how long it'll be before another chance like this comes up?"

The bell over the front door jangled as a matronly woman entered, followed by a slim man in a bowler hat. Penny slid her chair back. "I wish Campbell had come to you last June instead of a week before Christmas," she said, irritated. "Colorado Springs is a ghost town at Christmas time. Where are we going to find anyone to buy a one-third share in a copper mine?"

Before she could stand, Farley reached out to grab her hand. "That's not it, Penny. I think Willoughby Matthews may spring for it, but I have to convince him it's a good deal. I have the geology report, but I need an edge. Something that will pull Matthews in."

Penny pulled her fingers loose from his grasp. "Let me think about it," she told him. "I've got to wait on the Wilsons." She stood, smoothed her flowing skirts, and scooped a notepad from her starched apron pocket.

Smiling a welcome, she hurried to the first patrons for lunch that day, and Farley returned to the kitchen. Farley and their father, Michael, cooked and cleaned behind the scenes while Penny waited tables and tended the twelve-table dining room. During the peak season, Penny managed four waitresses. From September to May, she had no trouble working both shifts alone.

Farley's problem hovered in her mind. How could they convince Willoughby Matthews to turn loose his cash?

Matthews owned the Regal Astoria, one of the largest hotels in a town that catered to millionaires. Complete with hot-spring spas, riding stables, and suites the size of the Joshuas' entire house, the Regal Astoria had an international reputation. Willoughby Matthews could well afford to plunge a little. Unfortunately, he had a reputation for being inherently reluctant when it came to speculating.

Beginning at three that afternoon, Penny had two hours free before supper began. Bundling into her dark green coat and matching hat, she left the Joshua House of Fine Dining and headed toward the center of town. She wanted to get out into the air so she could think.

Daddy had opened the restaurant when Farley was ten and she was eight. Penny had been clearing tables and sweeping floors ever since. After Mama had died four years later, Penny had become a waitress at the restaurant six days a week. Later, she became Daddy's bookkeeper as well.

They lived comfortably, but they had no savings. What if something happened to Daddy? Farley didn't want to run the restaurant, and neither did Penny. She had other plans for her life, dreams of being a writer with a steady flow of royalty checks and fan mail. No one in the whole world knew about Penny's writing — she wasn't quite ready to share this dream with her family yet as she wasn't sure of their reactions — but she was a steady contributor to the *Colorado Springs Summit.* Writing under the name of Gregory Landis, she wrote novellas of five to ten chapters with one chapter printed each week. The paper was small, but she did get a penny for every ten words. It added up to as much as $2.50 a week, an amount she hoarded in a savings account. What she was saving for, she hadn't decided yet.

If only Farley could buy a share of the copper mine. He could marry Diane and they could have a life of their own without being tied to a commercial kitchen. Diane was a sweet, steady girl. She and Farley had been engaged for more than a year, but Farley wouldn't set a date. He wanted more for his bride than one cramped room over the restaurant, and he couldn't afford a place of his own.

She passed the grocer's shop and nodded to Mr. Connors. His delivery boy kept the Joshuas' restaurant supplied with a daily supply of goods.

What would give Willoughby Matthews

confidence that the copper mine was a good investment? Verbal promises wouldn't impress him. The geology report would help but . . .

A middle-aged gentleman in a dark suit passed her on the sidewalk.

Suddenly, she had an inspiration. What if Willoughby Matthews learned that someone else was investing in this venture? Someone Matthews would naturally respect?

"Hey! Wait up!"

Farley's voice behind her brought Penny to a stop in front of the Crabtree Feed and Grain Store. The sidewalk was littered with small bits of cracked corn and oats. She waited for Farley to reach her before she said, "What is it? Is something wrong?"

White gusts puffed from his mouth. He paused to catch his breath then said, "I need to talk to you." He took off his beaver hat and readjusted it on his head. "Have you thought of a way to get Campbell to come in on the deal?" he asked.

She reached out to take his arm. "Do you know of anyone else who's also investing?" she asked, falling in step with him.

He shook his head. "The Campbell Company works through silent partners. There's no published list of investors."

"Too bad. We could get one of them to go

with you to see Matthews. Just having someone important there would give you more credibility." They took four steps in silence. Her eyes narrowed as she gazed toward the steely sky. "Unless . . ."

"Sis? I get nervous when I see that look on your face."

"What if . . . what if we can find someone who *looks* important to go with you? What if Matthews only *thinks* the man is rich and backing the mine?"

Farley frowned at her. "That's dishonest. We could never get away with it."

"Can you tell a lie if you never open your mouth?" she challenged. "I don't mean to have someone spin a yarn to Matthews. All we need is someone who can make an impression without saying a word. You can introduce him as an associate and leave it at that."

He wasn't convinced. "It would take a lot of doing. You'd have to find someone willing, and then you'd have to bring him up to par — expensive clothes, the right bearing . . . and that's just the beginning."

Smiling at him like he was a three-year-old, she patted his cheek with her gloved hand. "Leave those things to me," she said. Looking both ways, she stepped off the sidewalk. "I'll be back by five." With short, quick steps she crossed the street and headed up the other side, leaving Farley staring after her.

Doing some quick mental calculations, she figured she had about fifty dollars to pull off the ruse. That should be enough. The problem would be finding a man who looked right and who would be desperate enough for some ready cash to go along with the plan.

Where could she find a well-formed-yet-poor man? He had to have a touch of aristocracy and good looks. Or did he? Well . . . he had to be intelligent, at least.

She turned into the main thoroughfare where the best hotels and restaurants lined the street. Maybe a waiter or a bellboy. Pulling her watch from her handbag, she quickened her pace. It was already four o'clock.

In the penthouse of the Olympia Hotel, twenty-six-year-old Justin Van der Meer adjusted his coat and black bowtie as he left his dressing room. He crossed the master bedroom and strode into a dining room glittering with gold and crystal.

Seated at a small table near the wide dining room window, his valet, Albert Wessel, looked up from his Parchessi game board and immediately stood. "Are you going down so early, sir?" he asked in clipped British consonants. He was an egg-shaped man, from his full-length silhouette to the form of his balding head. He had deep creases around his full mouth and twinkling brown eyes.

Reaching into his pocket for a small horsehair brush, he circled Justin's slim frame and swished at his dinner jacket, a tailored creation of pure lamb's wool with silk lapels.

"Why shouldn't I eat when I want?" Justin demanded with mock severity. "I'm hungry, and there's no one joining me. You know I'd much rather be alone in the dining room anyway, Vessel." For more than thirty years, Albert Wessel had been valet to Justin's grandfather, salt-mine multimillionaire Gustaf Van der Meer. Gustaf never lost his heavy Dutch accent, so Wessel had been "Vessel" to the family since the valet had traveled from Great Britain to join the Van der Meer household.

Waving the whisking brush away from his collar, the younger man approached the game board. "How is it going? Finish the tournament yet?" Since discovering Parchessi on their last trip to New York, the valet passed his every spare moment playing the game. When he couldn't convince anyone to join him, he played against himself.

"I'm on the last game," Vessel said, resuming his seat. "The far side is winning, 3-2. If the near side wins this round, we'll have to play a tiebreaker."

Justin laughed. "We? You're the only one playing," he said with a teasing light in his dark eyes. "Wouldn't you like to join me in the dining room for supper? No one will be there to see my *disgrace.*"

Vessel's reply was the gentle scolding reserved for a favorite son of the house. That's exactly what Justin had been until his grandfather's death the previous year. "Master Justin," he replied primly, slipping into Justin's old title, "it just isn't done."

"I know. I know." The younger man stepped away. He fluffed the back of his close-cropped hair with his fingertips and immediately smoothed it down. He paused to say, "I'll send you up a supper tray with some mulled cider and a big piece of cheesecake."

Vessel's expression brightened. "Very good, sir. Thank you, sir." He was back at his game before Justin closed the apartment door.

With his hands deep in his pockets and whistling a jaunty tune, Justin waited for the clanging, groaning elevator. His grandmother, Heidi, would have scolded him for the bad habits he'd picked up at Berkeley during the four years he'd lived in the dormitory. Remembering her guttural voice, he straightened and smoothed his coat.

Justin's father, Heinrich, was the only child of Gustaf and Heidi Van der Meer. Against his parents' wishes, Heinrich had married an actress with no social ties and little talent. When he contracted consumption less than two years after the wedding, Heinrich came home to be nursed by those he trusted and loved. His wife stayed only long enough to see her husband and their tiny son settled into the mansion. A few days later, she disappeared into the night and never returned.

All Justin knew of her was that her name was Rosalind, and she also died of consumption while she was in Europe. He was three years old at the time. All he had of his parents was an old tintype, too faded to make out their faces.

Gustaf and Heidi doted on Justin. They raised him with all the structure and strictness of their Christian Dutch heritage, determined that this boy would not become heedless and self-willed like his father. Justin grew up in a twenty-room mansion with leather-covered walls and priceless antiques, but he had few toys and no allowance. He had daily kitchen chores and worked in the stables on Saturdays.

Justin entered the empty dining room to the welcoming aroma of a well-cooked roast or stew. No waiter was in sight. He stepped toward the kitchen door, hoping to catch someone's eye, but no one appeared.

A few minutes later, he wondered if he should return to his room and come back in an hour. But what was there for him to do? Watch Vessel rolling dice and moving pawns? At least the scenery here was different. He had chosen Colorado Springs because it was off-season and he wanted some peace from the frantic partying of the young rich. With three days still remaining until Christmas, peace was beginning to seem horribly boring.

A crash in the kitchen startled Justin. He whirled around and backed into a large rack full of clean silverware. Lunging to catch it before it toppled over, he couldn't stop the disaster. The second crash followed close behind the first.

His face flaming, he bent over to salvage as much of the clean silverware as he could, carefully lifting those that had not touched the floor.

■ ■ ■ ■

Penny entered the lobby of the Olympia Hotel and looked around for prospects. The elderly gentleman behind the desk was certainly not a candidate for her purpose. No bellboys in sight. Moving across the wide, silent room, she entered the restaurant.

Was the entire hotel empty? Letting out a frustrated sigh, she turned to leave when a movement caught her eye. A tall, dark-haired young man was working over a silverware rack near the kitchen door. He was slim and had a straight set to his shoulders. Intrigued, Penny moved closer.

He must have felt the intensity of her stare because he turned to look at her before she reached him.

Penny's pulse quickened. He was handsome but not too pretty. Good carriage but not arrogant. He could have been an actor instead of a waiter. Maybe he would be before much longer.

Before she had time to second-guess herself, she strode up to him. "Good afternoon," she said breathlessly. "I have a job for you on Saturday at three o'clock. It will take about an hour, and I'll pay you twenty dollars." She paused and looked at him anxiously. "Do you have to work on Saturday?"

He gaped at her. "Excuse me, miss. Do you know me?"

"I'm sorry. I don't have time to wait for introductions. I need someone who looks rich to attend a business meeting at a high-class hotel on Saturday. It's at three-thirty. You won't have to say a word. My brother will introduce you to his associate. That's it. Do you want the job?" She scrutinized his jacket. "I'll have to find you something better to wear than that waiter's uniform, but I can manage that."

She paused to glance at his face, impatient now. "Will you do it? If you have to work that afternoon, I need to know right away so I can find someone else."

Dropping a handful of knives into a slot on the rack, the hint of a smile twitched his cheeks. He nodded in a highbrow fashion and said, "I'm free on Saturday, so that will be agreeable."

Penny let out a relieved sigh. She pulled open the top of her purse and found two coins. "Here's fifty cents. Get yourself a haircut and a shave and meet me at the Joshua House of Fine Dining this evening at eight o'clock. Do you know where that is?"

"I'll find it, Miss . . ."

"Penny Joshua," she said. "And your name?"

"Justin . . . Avery."

Stepping back, she looked him over again. "We'll need to work on you a bit, but I think you'll do fine." She gave him a glowing smile. "We'll see you at eight." Glancing at her watch, she rushed out.

The moment Penny disappeared through the doors, Justin sank into the nearest chair and began to laugh. Too well bred to shout or guffaw, he chuckled and chuckled until his eyes watered and his stomach ached.

He rubbed the two quarters together in his palm. What a lark. If only Teddy, Max, and the rest of the gang at Berkeley could see him now. It would have been the talk of the school for weeks.

Finally, a craggy-faced waiter emerged from the kitchen and approached his table. "May I help you, sir?" he asked.

Pulling out a handkerchief to wipe his eyes, Justin drew in a breath and tried to regain his composure. "Bring me whatever smells so good. It's beef, I think."

"Right away, sir." The waiter strode into

the kitchen.

Staring at six pairs of gold velvet drapes lined up on the opposite wall of the massive room, Justin savored the memory of a sweet pixie face, flashing eyes, and the most gorgeous blond hair he had ever seen. Suddenly, his boring Christmas holiday had become intensely fascinating.

CHAPTER 2

Justin finished his early supper in short order, chewing through a slab of succulent roast beef and gravy-covered mashed potatoes, barely tasting them. He ordered Vessel's meal, signed a bill, and headed for the street without his coat. The barbershop was just next door, and he didn't want to answer Vessel's questions about his sudden urge to go out.

Thirty minutes later, he returned to the hotel. He punched the button on the elevator, rocked on his heels, and chuckled again. Every time he thought of it, he had to laugh. Sometime between now and eight o'clock he had to get this laughing out of his system or he'd never make it through the evening. Miss Joshua would wonder if he'd had a drop too many if she saw him in this state.

Justin had always enjoyed a good joke. He picked up that trait from his many hours playing with stable boys, hearing the banter of the kitchen help, and playing dozens of games with Vessel. The old retainer had been like a second grandfather to Justin ever since he could remember — a favored grandfather because Gustaf was too involved with his business to be much fun. Vessel, on the other hand, had afternoons free to teach him croquet, whist, horseshoes, chess, and a ridiculous parlor game called Blind Man's Bluff, the house staff's favorite.

Entering the penthouse door, Justin tossed the key into a nearby crystal dish. Vessel's empty supper tray sat nearby, waiting for room service to pick it up.

Whistling, Justin headed for his room. He wanted a few minutes alone to compose himself.

However, when he passed Vessel's ongoing tournament, the older man cried out, "What — Ho! Sir, what happened to your hair?"

Justin stopped in mid-stride. He fluffed the bristly back of his head and smoothed it down. Pasting on a sober face, he slowly turned to the valet. "I stepped out and got a haircut," he said, as though it were a weekly event.

Vessel became instantly offended. "Master Justin, do you find my haircuts lacking in some way? All you have to do is tell me, and I will correct any deficiencies." He circled Justin to inspect the damage. "Is this your pleasure from now on? I'm not sure I can duplicate it. The back is too short, the crown stands up, and the front . . ." He craned his head for a closer look.

With his mind moving at lightning speed, Justin tried to come up with an answer that would satisfy the old fellow. Vessel had been cutting Justin's hair since he wore short pants. He forced a solemn look, knowing that it would squelch any further questions. He was, after all, the new master. "It's nothing I'm ready to discuss," he said shortly and quickly retired to his room.

He strode to the mirror to take a closer look at his head and winced. Inspecting from several angles the dark stubble covering his scalp, he picked up his brush and tried to comb it down. When he finished, it looked exactly as it had before. He set the brush back on the dressing table. Oh well, in a couple of weeks Vessel could put it to rights.

Penny skipped back to the restaurant. Excitement gave her wings. Her plan might just work after all.

Inside the back door, she shrugged out of her coat and pulled her hatpin from her narrow-brimmed hat. The cooking smells from that evening's menu — creamy onion soup and Beef Wellington — warmed the air. She placed her hat neatly on a shelf and hung the coat on a peg beneath it. Pausing to check her hair in a small mirror there, she hurried to the kitchen door and leaned inside. Their father was bent over the sink with his back to her.

She spotted her brother stirring a simmering five-gallon pot. "Farley," she called in a stage whisper and waved him closer.

Farley hooked the curved spoon handle over the edge of the pot and hurried to her. Stepping into the hall, he closed the door after him.

"I found him!" Penny bounced with every word. "He's going to meet us here tonight after we close."

Farley sucked in a quick breath. "You didn't!" He shook his head in warning. "I don't know about this, sis. You may be in over your head this time."

She grabbed his sleeve with both hands and shook it. "He's a waiter at the Olympia. He's a bit young, but he fits the part perfectly. And he said he'd do it for twenty dollars."

Farley frowned.

Turning him loose, she glanced at the

clock in the hall and set off toward the dining room. "I'm late setting up for supper," she said airily. "We'll talk about it later."

At six-thirty that evening, stretched out on his bed with his hands under his head, Justin Van der Meer was in a dilemma. He had to meet Penny in ninety minutes. If he wore his usual dinner clothes, her brother might spot him as a rich fraud straightaway. The problem was he didn't own anything shabby enough for a waiter's wardrobe, and every store in town closed by six, most shops by five.

He shifted the pillow a little lower and moved up to rest his back against the sewn-leather headboard. On the other hand, Penny had assumed that his two-hundred-dollar dinner jacket was a waiter's uniform. Maybe her brother would, too. That's the best he could do tonight. But tomorrow . . .

He hopped off the bed and crossed fifty feet of rose-covered carpet in shades of pink, crimson, and burgundy. "Vessel, I need you to do something for me tomorrow morning. The shops open at eight, don't they?"

Vessel stood and moved away from the game board. "Yes, I believe eight it is. What's your pleasure, sir?" The old retainer's gaze wandered over Justin's newly shorn head.

The younger man pulled a folded wad of bills from his pocket and peeled off several of them. "I know you're going to think it's strange, but please humor me." He fended off Vessel's expression of growing alarm with a wave of his hand. "It's just a lark. I don't want to go into it right now, Vessel, so please don't ask."

"Does it involve a pretty girl?" Vessel asked dryly, as he took the money from Justin's hand.

"As a matter of fact . . ."

Resigned and patient, Vessel replied, "Say no more, young sir. Say no more."

"I want you to find a cheap clothier and buy me a dark suit off the shelf. I'll need everything — shirt, shoes, hat, gloves, and overcoat. Well-cut if you can manage, but coarse, not fine."

"Very good, sir." Tucking the cash inside his vest pocket, Vessel returned to the Parchessi game. "We're in the tiebreaker. The far side has it so far, 3-1."

Justin inspected the board. "Would you like me to sit in for the far side?"

Vessel looked dutifully solemn. "If you will, sir."

Smiling, Justin backed away. "I just remembered I have a sketch to finish. Let me know when you're ready to start a new game."

Returning to his room, Justin chuckled. Vessel would rather cut off his nose than deny Justin anything, but coming in on the winning side at the end of the tournament would be like filching the last bite of the last piece of chocolate cake from his plate. The fact was Justin couldn't resist teasing the old fellow now and then.

Both Penny and Farley worked like Trojans to get the restaurant cleaned and in order before Justin arrived. Their father was scouring the monster stove in the kitchen.

"I hope he comes," Penny told Farley when he joined her in the dining room where she was filling small bowls with moist salt. All around her, chairs perched upside down on bare tabletops.

Rolling down his sleeves and buttoning them, he retorted, "I'm tired, and I need a bath. I almost hope he doesn't come."

"You ungrateful wretch." She picked up a neatly folded white napkin from a stack nearby and threw it at him. "I'm doing this for you, remember?"

He picked up the cloth napkin from where it fell at his feet. Holding it by opposite corners, he flipped it around to make a lumpy rope. Stretching it taut, he aimed it toward her arm. "Not for me, for us." With a teasing grin and a threatening gleam in his eye, he said, "Say it."

Completely unimpressed with his posturing, she said, "I know — for us." She grabbed the napkin away from him and dropped it into the canvas laundry bag propped nearby. It was stuffed with tablecloths and napkins. A young man from the Chinese laundry would come by to pick it up in the morning.

A knock sent her hurrying to unlock the front door. Pulling it open, she said, "Justin, please come in." A frigid gust blew her words back in her face and made her flinch.

Shivering in only his dinner jacket, he bounded inside. "Thanks for coming right away," he gasped. "I didn't realize how cold it was when I set off." He rubbed his hands together and blew on them.

"There's still hot coffee on the burner," Penny told him, closing the door and turning the lock. "I'll fetch you a cup." She waved toward her brother. "This is Farley Joshua, my brother, the one who got us into this."

She gave him just a second to shake Farley's hand, then said, "Let's use this table next to the radiator where it's warm," and hurried through the swinging doors into the inner sanctum of Joshua's House of Fine Dining. It had a massive Empire stove, a stone oven for baking bread, and three sinks on the left side. In the center stood a thick oak table and four chairs, and on the right was a long work counter lined with knife blocks and crocks filled with long-handled utensils.

With his enormous back bent over the stove, his meaty right arm in rhythmic motion over the black grill, Michael Joshua glanced over when Penny lifted the coffeepot from the far burner.

"A little late for that, ain't it?" he grunted.

"It's not for me, Daddy," Penny told him. "A friend just stopped by, and he's almost frozen. I thought this would warm him up."

"David Langstrom?" he asked slyly.

"Daddy! Why would *he* come over?"

He sent her a teasing smile. "You tell me, Penny."

Refusing to lower herself to answer such a ridiculous question, she turned her shoulder toward him and poured coffee from a gallon-sized enamel pot, emptying it. "Perfect. I always hate to waste it." She deposited the pot into a deep metal sink and left the kitchen. As the door swung shut, she heard her father's deep-throated chuckle.

David Langstrom was a deacon's son, just back from the university. Every unattached girl above the age of twelve had her cap set for him. Every one except Penny, that is. She thought David Langstrom was full of himself. She wanted a man who was more down to earth — kind and approachable like her dad.

She brought Justin's coffee to the table. "Please, sit down," she told Justin, who was still standing some distance away. She looked him over as he crossed the room. "See what I mean, Farley? That waiter's jacket won't do at all." She turned to Justin. "Do you have anything better than that?"

He looked at her with an uncertain expression.

Taking his hesitation for a no, she said, "I wonder if I can borrow one . . ."

Farley shook his head. "From whom?" he demanded. "That's why we're in this predicament, remember? Everyone's out of town."

"How could I forget?" she asked archly. She studied Justin's shoulders and said, "Stand up to Farley, so I can judge your size." She glanced from one to the other. "Just a tad narrower, I think. I'll take one of Farley's suits over to Bernard's in the morn-

31

ing and ask him if he has a ready-made suit the right size."

Taking a seat across from Justin, Penny said, "I hope you don't think we're awful for doing this. Farley has a chance to buy a large share of a new copper mine northwest of Denver. He's got the geology reports to prove it's a good investment, but he doesn't have enough money for a full share. He's looking for a backer to stake him for the rest of it in exchange for thirty percent of the profits." She paused to meet his eyes. "We're not trying to cheat anyone. It's just that our contact is so tight-fisted that we wanted a little extra persuasion to convince him to come in on the deal."

Justin turned to Farley. "Would you mind if I saw the report?"

Surprised, Farley shrugged. "Why not? It's all legit. I've got it in my jacket." He hustled into the hall and was back soon with a folded document.

He handed it to Justin, who looked over it.

Farley continued, "As you can see, there's no risk. The copper deposit is wide and deep. How can I lose?"

Justin slowly folded the report and handed it back. "You've got something there, Farley. It's worth pursuing."

Penny said, "We can't get anywhere without enough money." She smiled. "That's where you come in. We need your help, Justin. It means a lot to us."

CHAPTER 3

Justin grinned at Penny. She had the most fascinating almond-shaped blue eyes he had ever seen. "That's what I'm here for," he said. He glanced from her to Farley and back again. Pushing his empty cup away, he asked, "Where do we start?"

"Let's pretend that you're coming into the restaurant with Farley," she replied. "He'll introduce you to Mr. Matthews." Waving her hand toward the front doors, she said, "I'll be Mr. Matthews. Pretend to go outside and come back in."

The men walked most of the way across the dining room. When they were out of Penny's hearing range, Farley said, "You're a sport to do this, Avery."

"Twenty dollars is twenty dollars," Justin replied wisely.

With Farley leading the way, the men approached the table.

Penny stood and stretched out her small

hand. "How do you do, Mr. Joshua? It's good to see you."

Farley shook her hand. "Good afternoon, Mr. Matthews. I'd like you to meet my associate, Justin Avery."

Uncomfortable with the playacting, Justin hesitated.

Penny shook her head and gently scolded, "You're a millionaire, Justin. You're confident and relaxed. Mr. Matthews is just another man like you are, so don't act nervous." She sat down. "Let's try that again."

The men retired to the other side of the dining room. Farley put out a few of the gas lamps as they moved, leaving them in a pleasantly dim atmosphere.

When they had gone far enough, they stood waiting for her signal to approach. Farley sighed. "It could be a long night. When Penny gets her teeth into something, she's like a puppy going after an old sock."

"I'll try to get it right this time," Justin said and followed Farley's winding return path among the chair-topped tables. His elbow caught a leaning leg and the chair crashed to the floor, totally unnerving him. He stood staring at it.

Farley rushed back to pick it up. "Don't worry. These old things have seen more wear than a forty-niner's seen dirt." He set it back on the table.

Pulling his coat straight, Justin lifted his chin and drew in a slow breath. This time he minded his elbows and arrived at the table without incident.

"How do you do, Justin?" Penny asked, her voice extra deep.

Justin was quick to step up, look Penny in the eye, and firmly shake her tiny hand.

The men sat down, and Penny dashed to the hostess station for three menus. She came skipping back and dropped one in front of each place, then quickly resumed her seat and pasted on a blank expression.

In her deepest voice, she said, "I'll have the vichyssoise and coffee, please." She turned to Farley expectantly.

He cleared his throat, glanced at the cardboard in front of him, and said, "I'll have the same."

All eyes were now on Justin. He scanned the menu, and one item caught his eye. "Sauerkraut and sausages with boiled potatoes and kale," he said.

Penny stared. "You would go into a high-class restaurant and order *that*?"

Defensive now, he glanced at Farley. "It's one of my favorite meals. Why shouldn't I order it? Besides, what if I can't read the foreign words written on there?"

Penny's eyes narrowed. "How can you work at the Olympia Restaurant and not know the names of European dishes?"

He quickly explained, "I know the ones on that menu, sure. But both menus won't be exactly the same. I'd have to figure something out in a split second."

Actually, Justin was well read in Latin, French, and German, but he had to play dumb on this point. Besides, Grandma Van der Meer had believed that simple foods built strong bodies, so Justin had a distinct disliking for anything highly spiced, rich, or unrecognizable. He hardly looked at a menu whenever he ate out. He found it a boring waste of time when he had four or five favorites and almost always chose one of them.

With a sigh of great patience, Penny said, "What would you like, sir?"

Justin looked at her calmly and said, "I'll have the same."

Farley let out a loud hoot. "That's the best bet, old man. Whatever it is, we'll have to suffer through it."

Penny made a point of ignoring his sarcasm. "What about drinks?"

Justin held up his hands, palms outward. "I have a religious belief about temperance.

I've never tasted alcohol, and even twenty dollars isn't enough to get me to try it."

She looked at him, surprised. "Are you a Christian?" she asked.

"Yes, I am." Justin felt a blush coming on and despised himself for it. "I wonder if I shouldn't stop this charade right now," he faltered. "I want to help you kids, but . . ."

"Penny's a Christian," Farley told him. "She goes to meetings at the tabernacle north of town."

It was Penny's turn to look uncomfortable. "That's why I don't want you to tell any untruths, Justin," she said, glancing at her hands then upward toward him. "We're just trying to create an impression, not lead Mr. Matthews down the merry path. Farley has the geology report . . ."

"It's a good prospect," Justin broke in, glad for a valid reason to go ahead with their plan. "That's why I'm with you. You kids deserve a break."

Penny sighed. "I wish we had an actual meal so we could practice table manners."

Farley yawned. "Don't you think that's enough for tonight, sis? I'm beat."

She nodded. "Let's meet tomorrow at three while the restaurant is closed for the afternoon. Can you arrange that, Justin?" When he nodded, she went on, "We'll actu-

38

ally eat a meal together, so we can work on table etiquette." She gave Farley a pointed look. "You need practice on that as much as Justin does."

Farley groaned.

Pushing his chair away from the table, he stood, bade Justin good night, and trudged toward the back stairs.

Justin watched him go with a sinking feeling. He wasn't at all ready for the night to end.

"Daddy is finishing up in the kitchen," Penny said. "How about a cup of hot cocoa before you go back into the cold?" She seemed to have another thought. "You know, Farley has an old coat he uses to go out to the ice house. Why don't you borrow it until tomorrow? I can't stand to see you go back into that cold again. You'll catch something dreadful for sure."

"Why, thank you," Justin said, "for the cocoa *and* the coat. That's very kind of you."

She stood, and he did, too. He followed her to the kitchen door. When she paused just outside, he hesitated, uncertain of what she expected of him.

"A gentleman always opens a door for a lady," she said.

Feeling another blush coming on, Justin hurried to push the swinging door inward.

He'd been well versed in that bit of etiquette since he could walk, but he'd never seen it applied to a kitchen door before.

Once inside, Penny dropped all signs of pretense. "Daddy, this is Justin Avery," she said.

Michael Joshua was rinsing his grill stone under the faucet. He turned to greet Justin and then showed him his greasy hands. "I'd shake hands with you, but . . ."

"That's all right, Mr. Joshua," the young man replied with a smile. "Thank you for allowing me into your kitchen."

"We'd like some hot chocolate," Penny said. "Is the stove still hot?"

"That it is," her father replied. "There's still plenty of hot water in the reservoir, too."

The big man glanced at Justin with renewed interest, sizing him up, and Justin squirmed. He wondered if Penny's father had ideas about Justin's designs on his daughter.

Penny moved quickly around the kitchen, opening cabinet doors and lifting a small pot from a hook overhead. Watching her graceful movements, it occurred to Justin that Mr. Joshua might not be far off the beam.

In a few minutes, she had three warm cups on the oak table. "Can you sit down with us, Daddy?" she asked. "I've made a cup for you, too."

"You're a sweet child," he said, smiling sadly at Penny. Mr. Joshua washed his hands and wiped them on a towel. Pulling back the thick straight chair, he eased his wide girth onto the seat. "Penny is the image of her dear mother at that young age," he told Justin. "She was as blond as an angel and as tiny as a hummingbird."

"She passed away when I was twelve," Penny told him. She reached out to squeeze her father's hand. "Daddy's been mother and father to me and Farley. And a good job he's done of it, too." A warm look passed between them.

"My parents died when I was a baby," Justin said. "My father before I turned one and my mother when I was three. They both had consumption."

"How sad!" Penny said. She glanced at her father. "At least Farley and I both remember Mama." She spoke to Justin. "Who took care of you?"

"My grandparents raised me," Justin said. "They were good people."

"Were?" Penny asked.

He nodded. "Unfortunately, they were already old when I was born. They're both gone now."

"Do you mean you're going to be alone at Christmas?" Penny asked, alarmed.

"Well, we have an old family . . . friend . . . who has never married. I'm planning to spend the day with him."

She glanced at her father, then back at Justin. "Why don't you come and spend the day with us?" she asked. "We're going to be alone, too, the three of us, and it can be rather depressing. It would be fun to have someone in for a change." She turned toward her father. "Wouldn't it, Daddy?"

Setting down his cup, he looked blankly at his daughter for a moment then suddenly burst out, "Of course, of course. We'd be delighted to have you, young man."

Justin hesitated. "Would you mind if I bring my friend along? I'd hate to leave him all alone."

"That goes without saying," Penny told him. "Come early and stay late. Daddy cooks several turkeys for our Christmas Eve menu, and we enjoy the leftovers the next day. There'll be plenty to spare."

"That's kind of you," Justin said, feeling a strange warmth inside. "Very kind."

She beamed at him. "Did your family have any special Christmas traditions?" she asked. "We hardly do anything special for Christmas since Mama passed away. What did your family do?"

"My grandparents were from Holland, and they stayed with the Dutch traditions all their lives. We exchanged gifts on December 5 and only went to church on December 25."

"Did you do anything else on December 5?" Penny asked. The light of the lamp overhead shone in her eyes.

"We always had a huge tree lit with dozens of white candles," he said, smiling softly. "We'd string cranberries to wrap around the tree and then decorate the limbs with glass balls. And Grandma would always hide a pickle."

Penny wrinkled her tiny nose. "A pickle?"

He chuckled. "It was my job to find the pickle hidden among the branches. Then I'd get a special chocolate truffle all to myself."

"Did you always find it?"

"Almost always," he said. "When I was eleven, I couldn't find it because it was tied to the trunk under a wide branch. I was so disappointed that the cook . . ." He gulped. "That is . . . they cooked me a special cake the next day."

Penny sipped the last of her chocolate. "We used to make paper snowflakes and pinwheels and tie them to the tree with silk thread. And we'd string popcorn because Mama didn't like cranberries. She said they were too expensive and stained our clothes besides."

"You don't do that anymore?" Justin asked.

She patted her father's hand. "After Mama died, we just couldn't do the same things. Whenever I thought of pulling out the old Christmas decorations or putting up a tree, I wanted to cry. So, we never did." She smiled at her father. "What do you think, Daddy? Could we do some things this year?"

His fleshy face, so like Farley's, curved into a smile. "There's no harm in it," he told her, patting her cheek. "Do what you will."

She beamed at him, then turned to cast the glow of her smile upon Justin. "Tomorrow is Christmas Eve. We'll practice here from three o'clock to five o'clock then Farley and I will have to serve dinner. We close at seven thirty. Why don't you come around at eight? And bring your friend. It will be fun."

Her enthusiasm was contagious. "All right. I will."

Mr. Joshua got heavily to his feet, weariness in every move. "I'm going to write out my grocery order to leave for the delivery boy, and then I'm off to bed. You young people have to excuse the old man who needs his rest." With a wink for Penny, he pulled off his apron and disappeared through the swinging doors.

Justin pulled out his watch. Eleven o'clock. "I've kept you too late," he said, standing.

"Not at all." She smiled up at him. "I wonder that we haven't met before. Farley and I don't get out much, but we do know a lot of the food service staff in the hotel restaurants. Most of them have worked for us at one time or another."

Holding the kitchen door for her to pass, Justin left her comment unanswered. He'd almost tripped himself up once tonight. He didn't want to take a second chance.

Outside the door, she scurried down the hall and pulled a worn quilted coat from a peg and brought it back to him. "This is Farley's coat. You can wear it home and bring it back tomorrow."

"Thanks," he said, shrugging into it. The collar was worn through at the front edge, and it smelled of grease and old straw. But it was soft and warm. He buttoned it closely around his neck as they crossed the dining room.

At the door, Penny said, "Before work in

the morning, I'll see if Bernard has a suit that he'll let me rent for a day. That shouldn't cost too awfully much." She held out her hand. "Thank you for helping us, Justin," she said with a soft smile.

She gazed into his eyes, and Justin's world stood still.

The young girls in his circle were pampered and powdered, with agendas and innuendoes in every word, every action. This lovely creature was sweet and unspoiled, her only agenda to help her brother get a start in life.

And to think, if he hadn't knocked over that silverware rack, he might have never met her.

CHAPTER 4

A few seconds later, Penny locked the restaurant door behind Justin. She took her time crossing the dining room, shutting down each burning gas lamp as she came to it. Standing in the comforting dimness of the last lamp, she took a few moments to gaze into her memories of the evening.

Something about Justin Avery had captured her interest from the first time she met him. What was it? She couldn't quite tell . . . but he was charming.

Pulling a sheaf of paper from a locked cabinet below the waitress station, she found a pencil stub in her apron pocket and sat down to write. It was a new story about a tall young man with dark hair and lively eyes.

During his mad dash back to the Olympia penthouse, Justin shivered and scolded his feet for not moving faster. Even with Farley's coat, he was still freezing. His ermine-lined overcoat was much warmer, but it was also a dead giveaway, and he'd been forced to leave it behind. Vessel would have to find him a warm coat in the morning. He couldn't take this kind of punishment for the next three days without catching something dreadful.

Outside the hotel, he pulled the jacket off and turned it inside out. Rolling it into a bundle, he held it under his trembling arm and dashed indoors. Inside the hotel lobby, he strode to the elevator, still shivering in spite of the warmth cascading over him. What a wonderful thing central heating was. He made a mental note to have a system installed in the Milwaukee mansion right away. He rarely went there in the winter, but even the spring and fall were uncomfortably cool in that part of the country. He was scheduled to arrive there in March. Pulling a notepad from his inner pocket, he jotted a few words.

Vessel was in his own room when Justin reached the penthouse. The rooms were silent except for the slight hissing of a single gas lamp on the wall near the front door. Lit only by that lamp and a single candle in a brass holder, the apartment stretched out gloomily before him. Justin quickly turned off the gas and picked up the candle to find his way to his quarters.

He stowed the old coat in a back corner of his wardrobe and hurried out of his clothes. Within minutes he was soaking in a warm bath.

He started chuckling. Then he laughed loud and long. No sauerkraut and pork indeed. Was that more barbaric than eating snails and fish eggs? He let the hot water course over his face, soaking in the warmth. Penny Joshua was as cute as a blueberry muffin on a china plate. He could hardly wait to hear what sweet morsels would flow from her soft lips when he saw her tomorrow.

Say, since he was invited to their place for Christmas Day, didn't that mean presents, at least one for the family? What should he bring? He immediately imagined expensive hats and canes for the men and glittering jewelry or a fur wrap for Penny.

Shaking the water out of his eyes, he groaned. He was supposed to be a "poor man." He couldn't afford anything more than a few cents. And he had little time to shop. The stores would close at noon tomorrow. What was he going to do? Justin Van der Meer spent most of the night tossing and muttering to himself.

■ ■ ■ ■

Bernard had been friends with Michael Joshua since Penny was a small girl. He was Michael's mentor in business and his formidable chess opponent on cold, windy evenings. Penny reached Bernard's tailor shop at five minutes past eight the next morning, but she was still the second customer in the store. When she stepped inside, a portly man in a dark overcoat was staring at a dinner jacket and discussing something urgent with the tailor.

Bent and trembling, Bernard resembled a beaver standing on hind legs, wavering in the breeze. He wore a sagging suit with a cloth measuring tape draped around his neck and thick glasses on his wide nose.

"This is a very economical fabric," he was telling the customer. "Only fifty dollars for both coat and pants. The lining is cotton instead of silk, as you can see." He flipped back the hem of the jacket.

Interested, Penny stepped forward and stopped beside a rack holding twenty rolls of suit material.

"Is that the very cheapest suit you have?" the customer asked, doubtfully. "I'm actually looking for a coarser fabric than that."

With an affronted expression, the clothier straightened to his full height of five feet, three inches and smoothed the dark cloth with his shaking hand. "That's the cheapest, Mr. Wessel," he quavered, "though I can't imagine why Mr. Van der Meer would want something worse instead of better."

The patron glanced toward Penny and took a step toward the door. "I won't keep you, Bernard, when you have other customers. There has to be another shop in town that sells cheap suits."

Penny spoke up. "If you go three streets over to Fourth Avenue, there's a place called Maxine's. She may have what you need."

Bernard sniffed. "Imported from Mexico or China," he said. "Nothing for a gentleman there, Penny, my dear."

Penny raised her shapely eyebrows. "For your information, Mr. Bernard, my father buys all his suits there, and he looks just fine." Her sparkling eyes softened her rebuke. It was an old argument between the friends.

"Is that so?" the man asked, pleased. "I'll go right over. You say it's three streets to the west?"

"That's correct," she said, smiling sweetly.

"Good day, miss," he said, with a small bow from the waist. "Thank you for your kindness." He nodded toward the shop owner. "Bernard." With a nod, he placed his bowler hat on his round head and trudged away.

"Miss Joshua," Bernard wheezed, "what can I do for you this fine day?"

She stepped closer and held out Farley's best suit. "I brought this to judge the size. I want to rent a gentleman's suit for one day." She peered at him anxiously. "Is that possible?"

He hesitated, his rheumy eyes searching her face. "For anyone else, I'd say no. But for you, Miss Penny, I'll see what I can do. I don't have many ready-made outfits available." He held up Farley's jacket for a closer look.

"A bit narrower in the shoulders," she told him. "And a tad longer in the leg. The waists are about the same."

Leaving Farley's suit on a nearby table, Bernard disappeared through a curtained doorway. He returned a few minutes later carrying a jacket on a wooden hanger. "Someone ordered this one last fall and never came to pick it up." He shook his head. "I'll never understand. No matter how much money a person has, it's so wasteful to pay for something and not make arrangements to claim it."

He held the suit toward her for a closer look. "One hundred percent wool. Hand worked with a silk lining. You'll not get much finer than this." He looked at the pants. "I can take down the hem in a matter of minutes. The rest should fit fine."

"How much to rent it for one day only?" Waiting for the answer, she held her breath.

"The customer paid one hundred dollars to have it made. For one day? Ten dollars." The firm set of his lips told her that the price was not negotiable.

"I'll need a shirt and some shoes . . ." Now that she thought about it, the shoes Justin had worn last night would be fine for the meeting. "Just a shirt," she amended. "And a nice-looking necktie."

"Fifteen dollars," he said. "I'll have it all delivered to the restaurant by noon."

She pulled open the drawstring on her purse. "Thank you, Bernard."

"Tell your father to stop by some afternoon for a game of chess," he said. "I haven't seen him for months. He's got to take time to relax during the off-season. You can tell him that for me." He tucked the money into his jacket pocket and winked.

Penny smiled. "I'll tell him," she promised. "It would do him good to get away from the restaurant for a few hours." Since her mother's death, he spent more and more time in the restaurant until finally he only worked and then slept and awoke to do it again.

Pulling her coat closer about her, Penny huddled her neck deeper into the collar as she stepped into the winter wind. Well, that detail was taken care of. If she hurried, she still had time to borrow a copy of Thomas Hill's etiquette book from the pastor's wife.

Justin slept through breakfast. He'd lain awake into the wee hours of the morning, reliving the evening, laughing at the ludicrous situation, and mulling over images of Penny — the way she tilted her head, the sound of her voice, that delightful sparkle in her eyes. He rolled over to pull a pillow over his face and block out the sunlight.

It was no good. He had to figure out how to take a suitable Christmas gift to the Joshua home without spending a dime. Time was wasting.

The sound of the apartment door closing brought him full awake. Reaching for his dressing gown, he was at the bedroom door before Vessel reached the dining room.

"What do you have there?" Justin asked, eyeing a bulky package in the valet's hands.

"Your evening wear, sir," Vessel said in his

most proper voice. He always became irritatingly polite when he disapproved of something. "Straight from Mexico," he added. His voice took on the barest tinge of disdain. "It has a tag sewn in the back of the neck to say so . . . which I will remove immediately, of course."

"Is it that awful?" Justin asked with delicious horror.

Vessel handed him the bundle.

A few minutes later, Justin buttoned the suit jacket and turned in front of the full-length mirror. A double-breasted gray pinstripe, it was at the height of fashion about two years before. "Not bad. Not bad at all." He picked up the overcoat and slid into it. It was black and bulky, not fashionable but wonderfully warm.

"I got the entire ensemble from a place about six blocks from here," Vessel told him, pulling the back of the overcoat straight. "A young lady at Bernard's put me onto the place. It was a stroke of luck that she was there because Bernard had nothing that would have . . . pleased you."

Justin came alert. "A young lady?"

"She came in at a few minutes past eight, just after I did." He nodded. "An eyeful, that one."

The younger man turned to glance at Vessel. "Did you get her name?"

Standing back a little to frown at the overall effect of the suit, the valet said, "I remember it because it was unusual. Bernard called her Penny."

Justin paused, then casually unbuttoned the coat and handed it to Vessel. "Thank you, Vessel. Just order a light brunch because I'm going to dine early again today. That will be all for now, but we're invited to a Christmas Eve supper tonight at eight o'clock."

"*We*, sir?"

"Don't look so shocked," Justin said, grinning. "This isn't a gala affair. It's a light supper at the home of one of the restaurant owners in town. I recently met the family, and they are very nice people." He opened the wardrobe to pull out one of his own white shirts. "Don't be such a snob, Vessel," he told the valet. "We'll have a wonderful time."

"Master Justin," Vessel said, exasperated, "when are you going to tell me what you are doing? You must be careful. Your status —"

"Can be a real bore," Justin finished. He chuckled and sent a Cheshire-cat grin toward the old man. "Don't worry. I'm having the time of my life. When you meet the

Joshua clan you'll see what I mean."

He finished unbuttoning the new shirt and threw it on the bed. Vessel picked it up. Justin was slipping his arms into the sleeves of his own shirt when he noticed Vessel's disturbed expression. "All right," he said. "I guess I'll have to fill you in before we go over there this evening." He nodded toward a chair. "You may as well sit down. This will take a few minutes."

CHAPTER 5

Vessel moved into the blue wingback chair a short distance from the bed. He wore a slightly worried expression but didn't say anything more.

Justin finished dressing in a leisurely manner as he spoke. He started the tale at the beginning with his visit to the hotel restaurant on the day before and ended with Penny's invitation.

"We're supposed to be there at eight o'clock for supper," he finished.

Vessel continued to watch Justin's face without speaking. He simply sat there with his hands on his lap, unmoving.

Justin tied a white satin scarf loosely around his neck and pulled on a black smoking jacket, his morning loungewear. Shoving his hands deeply into his pockets, he did a complete turnaround to survey his room.

"I need you to help me out, if you don't

mind," he said, ignoring Vessel's quiet disapproval. "I have no gift to give the family on Christmas morning, and I can't spend any money without giving myself away."

Vessel sniffed. "It seems you've put yourself in the position of the vast majority of all the world," he said. "They manage to figure out a solution. I'm sure you will, too." With that he stood and politely left the room.

Justin pulled out his bureau drawers and fingered through their contents. He'd brought five large trunks with him to Colorado Springs, but now they seemed so little. If only he were at home in Nevada, he'd have unlimited options for trinkets to give away. As it was . . .

Almost an hour later, he gave up in despair. A fellow couldn't give just anything to a family . . . all right, a girl . . . he'd met only recently. Frowning and chewing his lower lip, he opened his teak jewelry case looking for some bauble that might serve. Finally, he let the lid drop. Nothing there.

He opened his closet doors and stood back. Every item hanging inside was purchased for a specific purpose that was very male. Nothing there either.

He flung himself back on the bed with his hands clasped behind his head. What did a fellow give a girl he was interested in, one that would please her and yet be casual enough so as not to scare her away?

After obtaining the etiquette book from the pastor's wife, Penny Joshua continued her morning errands. She was looking for Christmas treats and some gifts. She stopped at the bank to make a small withdrawal from her secret savings account. For three years she had hoarded her magazine paychecks with no specific purpose in mind. Occasionally she would make a withdrawal for a pair of shoes or some gloves when she needed them.

Penny visited the local grocer, Mr. Connors. When she arrived, he was putting the final oranges on a tall display of Christmas apples and oranges in a bin just inside the front door.

Tall and lanky with a craggy face and beard that made him look something like Honest Abe, the shopkeeper looked up when the bell on the door jangled.

"Good morning, Penny. What brings you out so early?"

Penny smiled. "Merry Christmas, Mr. Connors. I've come to fetch some things for our Christmas dinner." She looked at the oranges and apples. "Those look so good. How much are they?"

"A penny apiece. That's a new shipment of oranges just come in from California. And are they good! The apples are some I've had in cold storage, but they're still crisp and sweet."

"I'll take six oranges," she said, feeling extravagant and liking it, "half a pound of popcorn, and a gallon of apple cider." She handed him her basket and walked toward the end of the counter to peer into a thick glass crock. "Is that cinnamon?" she asked, delighted.

Adding oranges to the basket, he nodded. "Bought 'em from a peddler last week. The feller always comes around before Christmas with a sack full of spices from the Orient. If you're interested, you'd better get some while you can. They won't last long."

She looked at the small square card in front of the crock reading, "5 Cents/Stick," considered for three seconds, and plunged. "I'll take one stick of cinnamon," she said and moved on. Her father kept cinnamon in a locked cabinet. He'd never allow her to use even a smidgen for the family. That would be eating up the profits.

Her shoes sounded loud on the floor as she circled the U-shaped counter, looking for gifts. This year she wanted four instead of two. Finally, she decided on three items.

"Anything else, Penny?" Mr. Connors asked as he wrapped her choices.

"That will be all," she said, pulling at the strings on her purse. "Can you have those things sent around to my house in about two hours? Not the restaurant, the house. If they go to the restaurant kitchen, there'll be no surprises on Christmas morning." She grinned as she handed him some coins and lifted her heavy basket from the counter.

Dropping the money into a metal box with small dividers in it, Mr. Connors smiled and his beard grew wider. "Tell your old dad to stop by and shoot the breeze sometime. All I ever see of him anymore is the grocery list the delivery boy brings in."

Penny smiled. "I'll tell him." She tucked her small cloth purse into a deep pocket hidden in the folds of her skirt. "Have a wonderful Christmas. And tell Mrs. Connors I said hello."

"The same to you and yours!"

Penny let herself out and headed up the street. She'd always tried to get a little gift for Farley and her father, but she wanted this year to be special. It was the first year since her mother died they'd actually had Christmas dinner with all the trimmings and guests as well. Maybe she could talk Farley into cutting them a tree this afternoon. Wouldn't it be fun to decorate a tree tonight? She and Farley . . . and Justin? The image brought a soft smile to her face and made her feet move a little faster.

She spent the next hour completing her shopping and arrived home in plenty of time to hide her bundles. She placed two long, slim sheets of stiff paper on her dressing table. This evening she'd cut out the printed forms and sew together four ornaments, ornate six-sided spheres with a different winter scene on each side. She'd gotten them for a steal and couldn't resist.

Glancing at the clock on the mantel shelf in her room, she hurried to her chifforobe to find a clean work dress. She had to be in the dining room in thirty minutes.

At five minutes past three that afternoon, Farley unlocked the door to let Justin into the restaurant.

Stepping inside, Justin handed him the old coat that he'd borrowed the night before.

"Thanks," Farley said. "That was perfect timing." He turned it around and slid his arms into it. "I'm going out," Farley told him with a look of intense relief. "Penny has it in her head that we need a Christmas tree to decorate tonight, and I am the one to find it, chop it down, and bring it home."

His grin showed that his next words were totally insincere. "I'm awfully sorry. You'll have to face the lion alone. Don't let her wear you out, old man. You have my sympathies."

He re-opened the door and paused to say, "I'm picking up Diane, my fiancée, on my way out of town." With another delighted grin, he sent Justin a nodding salute and closed the door firmly behind him.

Not at all disappointed, Justin unbuttoned the front of his new overcoat as he crossed the dining room. The afternoon had just become promising.

Penny stepped through the swinging doors and stopped, watching him critically as he moved toward her. "Would you do me a favor?" she called.

Justin paused in mid-stride. That was an unusual way to greet a guest. Should he say hello or answer her question?

She didn't wait for his response. "Would you mind going back to the door and walking in again? I'd like to look at your deportment before you take off your coat. And please don't unbutton until you reach the coat room attendant."

She was all business, that one. Pulling in his lips and pressing them together while he had his back to her, he did his best to stifle the smile that was determined to betray him.

Careful to keep his chin up and his expression blank, he made it back to her without having to do a third run.

"May I take your coat, sir?" Penny asked, primly.

"Thank you," Justin said carefully. He loosened his buttons with methodical accuracy, shrugged out of it, and handed it to her carefully folded over one arm.

She took the coat by its collar and hung it on a peg nearby. "Your table is ready. Please follow me." She led him to the same table where they'd practiced the night before. It was set up with two meals: baked chicken on a bed of rice with some kind of cabbage salad and green beans.

Moving quickly, Justin stepped behind a chair and pulled it out, bowing slightly toward her to show that he would like to seat her.

Penny looked surprised and at a loss for moment, but she quickly recovered and sat down with a murmured "Thank you."

Justin took his own seat across from her and looked into her gorgeous eyes. Had it been sixteen whole hours since he'd seen her last? It seemed like a lifetime.

She lifted her napkin, shook it out, and

draped it over her navy skirt. Justin imitated her actions. He picked up his fork two seconds after she did, tasted when she did, and then complimented the meal.

Without touching the chicken with their fingers, they carefully pried up tiny bits of flesh with their forks. The entire process was intensely tedious. He could understand Farley's glee at being excused.

It was a challenging game to see how long he could continue without her rebuke. His grandmother had been a stickler for table etiquette. Since he was a small child, Justin had been schooled in which fork to use, what to say to a lady at the dinner table, and the proper expression reserved for servants in the dining room. Of course, at Berkeley he'd relaxed some of that after being with the American students who knew nothing of the strict Dutch society he'd grown up in.

In the year since he'd inherited the family fortune, he'd been amazed at the rude, uncouth behavior of about half the rich people he came in contact with. They seemed to think that their money gave them the right to be unpleasant. In Justin's mind, acting like a millionaire meant flinging cigar ash over everyone and everything within range, shouting orders, and being outrageous when the mood hit.

Fifteen minutes later, they were deftly scooping the last grains of rice from their plates and discussing the weather in excruciating detail.

When Justin drained his coffee cup, Penny asked, "Would you like another cup? We're having Napoleons for dessert, Farley's specialty. Daddy sent him to a French cooking school in New Orleans last year."

"Thank you. I believe I will have another cup of coffee."

She hurried away and returned with a tray holding two dessert plates and the coffeepot. She served the food, poured coffee, and hurried away with the pot.

Justin waited for her to join him before touching the food.

When Penny returned, he quickly stood to seat her again.

"Thank you, Justin," she said sweetly. "You're doing amazingly well. All you need to work on is your enunciation. From time to time I hear a sort of guttural tone to your words."

Justin stiffened. "As I said, my grandparents were from Holland," he told her. "They both spoke with a heavy Dutch influence to their pronunciation. We also have a good friend who is British. I'm afraid I picked up some of each accent — a curious combination, but I'm stuck with it."

She nodded. "Well, that's all right. It's not a major problem."

He hid a sigh of relief. There was nothing he could do about the way he spoke. After all the teasing from his friends at college, he'd tried to talk more like they did and succeeded to a degree, but his Dutch heritage would be with him for the rest of his life. He'd had to accept that years before.

She took a careful bite of her pastry. Swallowing and touching her mouth with her napkin, she asked, "I haven't seen you around Colorado Springs before. Where are you from originally?"

"Nevada. My grandfather was in mining there until he died last year."

"He was a miner?" Penny asked. "No wonder you were interested in Farley's report. Have you done any mining yourself?"

Skating on thin ice, he decided to stall. He didn't want to tell any lies, but she was making it very difficult. "Tell me about your mother," he said. "She must have been a very special person to have such creative and responsible children."

"She was," Penny said softly. "She was very hard-working. She helped Daddy build this restaurant." She looked around at the green-flocked wallpaper, the tin tiles on the ceiling, and back to him as she went on. "She'd hold while he nailed. She'd plumb while he set a stud. They were always together. That's why my dad has been so lost since she's been gone. He's never been able to get his feet under him again."

"I kind of know how he feels," Justin said, unable to hold back the sadness in his voice. "First my grandmother passed away and six months later my grandfather. I guess I still feel like I'm drifting. They left me the family house in Nevada, but I don't go there much. Staying there feels like sleeping in a museum. It's nice enough, but empty and cold."

Penny nodded. "Without the Lord's help, I don't know how I would have survived," she said. "Neither Farley nor Daddy is a Christian. Mama was, though. She loved the Lord, and she made me promise that I would keep a Christian testimony in the house."

Her eyes filled with sudden tears. "I don't know what it will take for Daddy and Farley to accept Christ. I know Daddy wants to be with Mama more than anything in the world, but he won't humble himself and ask Christ to save him. Whenever I mention anything about the Lord to him, he puts me off by saying he's tired or he's too busy to talk about it right now."

Justin wanted to reach out and comfort her more than anything he'd ever wanted in his life.

With a chagrined look, she dabbed at her eyes with her fingertips. "I'm sorry. I didn't mean to get all weepy on you." She sipped her coffee. "Tell me, what are your plans? Surely you don't want to be a waiter all your life."

A short laugh burst from Justin's lips. Quickly, he swallowed to stifle the mirth. "You're right about that. I've never wanted to be a waiter." He grew more serious. "Actually, I haven't come to the answer of that question. What are my plans? My grandfather took it for granted that I'd follow him in mining, but I'm not sure that's the best for me."

He hesitated for just a second then plunged ahead. "My real passion is art. I was an only child, and I spent many hours alone. When I was drawing, the time would go so quickly that I'd hardly realize it. My grandparents thought art was a useless pastime, totally unworthy of being a profession, so I've never pursued it."

"What medium do you use?" she asked.

Intrigued at her knowledge of the subject, he said, "Pencil and charcoal, sometimes alone and sometimes together." He warmed to the subject. "I like doing landscapes and animals. I'd spend hours in the stable sketching the horses, the dogs, and the cats out there."

He set down his fork. "I took a couple of classes without my grandparents' knowledge. I didn't like sneaking around to do it, but something inside me made me press ahead." He grinned like a bad schoolboy. "I have to admit that I loved every minute of it."

Her eyes alive with interest, she asked, "Do you have any of your drawings with you?"

Embarrassed now, he shrugged. "I have a couple of sketchbooks in my room. I've never shown them to anyone. They're probably not very good."

"An artist never values his own work, unless he's extremely arrogant," she said. She rested her forearm on the table. "Would you mind bringing some of your works with you tonight? I'd love to see them."

He drew back a little. "They're probably not very good, Penny. You'll be disappointed."

Her lips drew together in a daring expression. "How about if we make a deal?" She paused then quickly said, "If you'll show me your drawings, I'll show you my . . . writing."

"Your writing?" He tried not to be shocked. It wasn't unheard of for a woman to write for publication — Louisa May Alcott and Harriet Beecher Stowe had been very successful — but he was having a hard time fitting this new piece of information in with the young woman who sat across from him. He focused in on her and lowered his voice. "Do you mean stories for your family?"

Her chin lifted a fraction. "I mean stories for the newspaper. That's all I'm going to tell you now. Bring your sketchbooks tonight, and you'll get the rest of the story."

He shook his head, smiling at her audacity in spite of himself. "Farley was right. When you get your teeth into something, you don't let go."

"Do we have a deal?"

He held out his hand to shake. "Deal. But no one sees them except you."

She clasped his hand in a firm grip. "Agreed, under the same conditions." She smiled, the victor. "The restaurant closes early because it's Christmas Eve, so we'll have dinner at seven thirty." She gave him an arch look with a teasing smile. "Be sure to bring your friend along and don't be late."

CHAPTER 6

At quarter to five, Justin headed back to his hotel with his head whirling and his heart thumping like the pistons on a steam engine. Show his drawings to a girl he'd only met a couple of days ago? Before he met Penny, he would never have considered it. But today, he was excited at the prospect. Would she like his work? Somehow he knew she would, and it had nothing to do with the sureness of his lines or the delicateness of his shading.

Vessel was still tiresomely polite when Justin reached the penthouse. Ignoring him, Justin retired to his room and closed the door. He had too much to think about for the next two hours. And he had yet to come up with a suitable gift for that lovely girl.

He looked through his trunk for the fifth time. Bother! Nothing would suit. What was he going to do? Unless . . . His gaze paused on something on top of his dressing table.

Lunging to his feet, he swiped it up with a delighted gasp.

Penny was setting up the waitress station for the dinner crowd when Farley swept in from the cold, his cheeks and nose brilliant red.

She set down the spoon she was holding and dashed toward him.

"What's with you, sis?" Farley demanded, pulling off his coat. "I'm the one who's been freezing in the cold woods, but you have rosy cheeks just the same."

With a small giggle, she pressed both palms against her face. "Did you get it?" she asked.

"A tree?" he replied, delaying his answer.

"Farley!"

"Yes, Miss Joshua. I cut down a spruce up on Blackbird Hill. It's about five-and-a-half feet tall." Pulling off his coat, he showed her his scratched wrists. "That thing was a bear. I had an awful time loading it on the wagon. If it weren't for Diane's help . . ." He clamped his jaw shut.

"Diane?" She pushed him in the chest. "Now who's holding out? No wonder you didn't complain about going!" She peered out the window of the back door. "Did you take her home already? I'd like to see her.

We haven't talked for ages."

He nodded. "Her parents are having lots of family over for dinner tonight so she had to get home. I may slip over there later this evening and say my howdys."

"See if you can bring her back with you for a few minutes," Penny said. She reached up to kiss his cheek. "You're a dear." She turned away to rush back to her work, calling over her shoulder, "Daddy's waiting for you to cut the pies. You'd best get moving."

The moment Penny unlocked the restaurant door, a dozen people poured inside — two couples and a family of eight. She stayed busy until the moment the last party went out at fifteen past seven.

Justin would arrive in fifteen minutes and she absolutely had to change clothes. Propping open the swinging doors, she called to her father and brother, "When Justin knocks, let him in. I'm going upstairs." Holding her skirts high, Penny made her way up the narrow steps with practiced grace and flew to her bedroom.

The family quarters were located over the restaurant with stairs both outside and inside. With three bedrooms and a modern bath, it was very comfortable. The kitchen was a tiny galley with only the barest essentials. But that was no problem for them since they ate at the restaurant three times a day.

Her dress, made from a dark green fabric with creamy white lace at the collar and cuffs and a green-and-red plaid sash around the waist, was hanging on a peg. As she was tucking up her hair, she realized she was excited about seeing Justin again.

Justin was dressed in his cheap suit and ready to leave at six forty-five. He stepped into the dining room and drew up when he saw Vessel still in his shirtsleeves and playing Parchessi.

"Vessel, we'll need to leave in thirty minutes," he said, worried. "You'll have to hurry so we won't be late."

The valet stood up, very straight, with his expression completely composed. "Begging your pardon, sir, but —"

"No, I'm begging," Justin interrupted. "*Please* come with me this time, Vessel. I'm asking you . . . please."

Vessel regarded the young man's face for a moment. "As you wish," he said and headed for his room. Ten minutes later, he reappeared wearing his dinner jacket, his overcoat on his arm.

They left without any further conversation. Carrying his sketchbooks in a thin leather case, Justin led the way, relieved to have Vessel with him. He wanted the old fellow to meet the Joshua family. Why it was so important to him, he didn't analyze. He just knew it was important.

When they stepped out of the clanking elevator and into the hotel lobby, a blond young man in a dark suit left the lobby desk and headed toward them. "Justin!" he cried. "I was hoping to catch you!"

Justin lost his breath for a moment. "Teddy!" he finally managed to croak. "What are you doing here?" Teddy Criswell was his old roommate and best friend from Berkeley.

Teddy shook his head and grimaced. "You won't believe what's happened to me since I saw you last summer."

"How did you find me?" Justin asked, still breathless.

"I sent a telegram to your house in San Francisco and got a reply that you were here." A faint note of desperation made his words sound tense.

Justin finally keyed in on what he was saying. "Are you in trouble, old man?" he asked.

"Not in trouble, no." His face became downcast. "I was in Denver to spend the holidays with Alice. I was all set to propose tomorrow morning. Had it all planned." He pulled a velvet box from his vest pocket and waved it toward Justin. "Then out of the blue she ended our courtship this morning. What was I going to do? Hang around her house for three more days? Not on your life." He shoved the box back into his pocket. "When I found out you were so close, I caught a stage."

"Teddy," Justin said, trying to think fast, "we're going out for a dinner engagement. Would you mind getting supper in the hotel here and waiting for me in our rooms?"

The other man nodded. "That's fine with me. I'm beat. A hot bath and a comfortable bed sound like heaven to me."

Justin handed him the key to the penthouse. "Vessel has a spare key to let us in later. Take the green room. Third door on the left of the hall."

"You're the greatest, Justin," he said, taking the key. He turned toward the dining room then turned back. "Who are you dining with?" he asked. "I thought no one was in town this time of year."

Ignoring Vessel's baleful stare, Justin said, "We'll talk about it later, Teddy. It's too complicated to go into now. I'll check in on you when we get back."

He headed toward the door with Vessel

close at his heels. As they reached the tall outer doors of the hotel, Justin could have almost sworn he heard a *harrumph* from the valet, but Vessel was too well bred for that.

Teddy was a good sport and a lot of fun. He was also a great tease. He and Justin had played their share of pranks while they were at school together. The son of a moderately wealthy family who owned a chain of farm equipment stores, Teddy had majored in agricultural science. They had a standing joke that both he and Justin loved to dig in dirt: Justin for what he could get out of it and Teddy for what he could put into it.

When Justin first met Teddy, they were freshmen at Berkeley. The senior men had painted thin slabs of wood to match the school's restroom doors. They'd carefully covered the "WO" portion of the word women and then stood aside to watch the fun. Justin was headed inside when he met Teddy — red as raw beefsteak — bolting out to a chorus of shrill screams. The seniors had laughed themselves silly, but Justin had never mentioned the incident to Teddy since. Some things are just too painful.

If it hadn't been for Justin's involvement with the Joshua family, he would have been delighted to see his old friend, Teddy. As it was, he felt a nervous twitch in his left jaw that wouldn't go away.

When Justin and Vessel arrived at the restaurant, Farley opened the front door, stepped out, and closed it behind him. He was carrying a lantern. "Let me show you how to get to the entrance of our apartment," he said, leading the way down the gravel-covered alley next to the building. "Then you'll know where to find our front door when you come again."

At the back corner of the structure, he turned left. The stairs slanted away from the building, and they reached the bottom step ten paces later.

Justin kept glancing back at Vessel, marching steadily after him for twenty stair risers. The older man never paused or changed his stoic expression. Justin was beginning to worry. He hadn't seen Vessel this reserved since Grandfather had sent him to Berkeley with a letter for the dean in an attempt to stave off a suspension threat.

During their sophomore year, Justin, Teddy, and their third roommate, Matt Jenkins, had greased every doorknob in North Hall, including the outer doors, and had ground the entire male student body to a halt. Not that the men had cared. They thought it was a lark, but the faculty was livid. Every first-hour class had started late.

Farley stepped into the apartment with Justin and Vessel behind him. They stopped in the front hall to take off their coats. Farley did the honors and then led them into the parlor. "My father's putting together our dinner and dealing with tonight's leftovers," he said. "I'd better help him out. Would you mind waiting here? Penny should be with you in a few minutes."

Justin made the right response and found a chair. Vessel did likewise and remained as still as a stone. Propping the leather case against the leg of the chair, Justin looked around.

The parlor was large enough for a short camel-backed sofa and three chairs with a secretary and a chest of drawers against two of the walls. A large alcove with four mullioned windows added light and space. Crocheted doilies and antimacassars covered almost every surface, even the arms of the chairs. A delicate hurricane lamp with a milky glass shade stood on a spindly round table in the center of the alcove, creating a gentle glow. It would have been a perfect subject for a still life, with the white gauze curtains billowing behind it.

On the other side of the room stood a dining table, already set for dinner with a white tablecloth and gold-rimmed china. The table had six Windsor chairs around it.

The men had been seated for a few moments when Penny entered the room. Her glossy blond hair shone against the dark green fabric. Lurching to his feet, Justin had to guard himself from staring. Every time he saw her she seemed more beautiful.

"Good evening, Justin," she said, beaming at him as she shook his hand. "I'm so glad to see you." She glanced at Vessel, who was also standing.

"This is Albert Wessel," Justin said.

Smiling a delighted welcome, she offered him her hand. "Mr. Wessel, how good of you to join us this evening." She took a seat on the plush sofa, and the men sat down in chairs across from her.

Penny told them of the Christmas tree that Farley had cut. "After supper, we'll haul it up here and put it in the alcove." She nodded toward the hurricane lamp. "I'll have to find another spot for that."

A knock at a nearby door brought Penny to her feet. "That's the men with the food," she said. She crossed the room and pulled open a door in the hall. Farley stepped through carrying a large platter of turkey with a bowl of stuffing balanced on top of it.

"Dad's behind me with a tray," he said, puffing a little. "I'm ready to say we should have eaten downstairs."

"Don't be a spoilsport," she chided. "We eat there every day of the year. Why can't we enjoy our own home for a change?"

Justin stood. "Can I help carry anything?"

Michael Joshua stepped into the hallway and nodded. "There's a pitcher of tea on the kitchen table," he wheezed.

Glad for something to do, Justin hustled down the steps and was soon back with the metal pitcher.

The five of them gathered around the table, and Penny introduced Vessel to her family.

"Please call me Vessel," he told them. "Everyone does."

Hearing the friendly note in the valet's voice, Justin sent a sly glance his way and caught Vessel softly smiling in Penny's direction while she talked to her father.

Justin stifled the urge to give the older man a nudge in the ribs. After all his disapproval, she'd smitten him, too. If that didn't beat all.

He must have been grinning, because Penny turned toward him and gave him an inquiring look. Sobering, he bowed for prayer as Mr. Joshua said the blessing.

When they raised their heads, Penny lifted a bowl of mashed potatoes and handed it to Vessel. "Tell me, Mr . . ."

"Vessel," he repeated, smiling at her. "No mister. Just Vessel."

"Yes, um, Vessel, how do you like Colorado Springs this time of year?"

"The mountains are beautiful," he said, taking the dish from her hand. "But it's too cold for my liking, and too windy. I much prefer California."

"California?" she looked at Justin.

He looked at Vessel.

"I lived there years ago," Vessel said. "I like to go back to visit from time to time. Have you ever been there?"

"I haven't had the pleasure," she said.

Mr. Joshua added, "It's a dream of Penny's to see the ocean." He passed the platter of turkey. "Me, I'm content to stay at home."

"Justin tells me you're an old friend of his family," Penny said. "Are you in mining, too?"

Feeling his way along, Vessel slowly replaced his glass on the table.

"I told her about my grandfather being in mining," Justin told him, "and how he wanted me to follow in his trade."

"I'm in men's clothing," Vessel said, moderately dignified without being too stuffy.

"That's where I saw you!" Penny burst out. "Bernard's shop. I knew you looked familiar."

CHAPTER 7

Justin felt a surge of alarm.

"Did you find a proper suit for Mr. Van der Whoever?" Penny asked Vessel. "Bernard is a wonderful tailor, but he's so expensive."

"We're old chess players," Mr. Joshua added. "I haven't had a good game with Bernard for ages. Too long."

"He said to come by in the evening and have a game," Penny told him. "You really ought to, Daddy. It would do you good."

"Have you ever played Parchessi?" Vessel asked Mr. Joshua, his smooth face hopeful.

The big man frowned. "What did you call it?"

"Parchessi. It's the royal game of India, just come to the U.S. of A. It's marvelous fun."

"You don't say. I've never heard of it."

Vessel described the game in detail, finishing with, "It's a wonderful pastime."

Justin chuckled. "He ropes me into a game whenever he can. I'm sure he'd love to have some new competition."

"It sounds very interesting," Michael said, intrigued. "I'd love to try it."

"After the meal, why don't I go round and fetch the board?" Vessel asked. "It's just a few minutes' walk to my quarters."

"I'd hate for you to venture out in the cold and dark to get it," Penny said.

"Not at all, my dear. I'd be delighted."

Justin smiled to assure her. "He means it, Penny. It would be the highlight of his holiday."

"In that case, please do." She beamed at him again.

Vessel's smooth cheeks flushed a little.

Farley finished the last of his sweet potato and raised his napkin to his lips. "Sorry to be rude, but I've got to run. Diane is expecting me."

Penny laughed. "We wouldn't dream of keeping you," she said. "Not that we could if we tried."

He gave her a pat on the shoulder and headed for the outside stairs. "I'll be home before midnight," he called just before the door banged after him.

Mr. Joshua grunted. "He's young and in love. You'll have to excuse his manners." He helped himself to a second helping of potatoes.

When they finished the meal, Justin helped Penny clear the table and carry the dishes back to the restaurant kitchen. Vessel set out for the hotel, and Penny's father retired to his room for a much-needed break while he awaited Vessel's return.

Downstairs, Penny ran hot water into the deep metal sink while Justin scraped and stacked, an art he'd learned from his duties in the mansion's kitchen. Before long, they had a system in place and the dishwashing progressed with speed.

"I've got your suit," Penny said. "Bernard sent it over this afternoon. He's going to let me keep it until the meeting and only charge me for one day."

"Nice of him," Justin said, wiping a cup.

"You can take it home with you this evening, if you'd like," she said. They worked in comfortable silence for a few minutes. "Did you bring your sketches?" Penny asked, handing him the last plate to dry.

"Of course," he said, smiling into her eyes.

"In that case, I'll show you my writings before we go up. I keep them locked in a cabinet down here. My menfolk wouldn't dream of looking through the waitress station, you know."

Drying her hands, she led him through the swinging doors. He found a seat at their usual table while she fetched the pages.

He'd expected handwritten sheaves of paper, but she brought him copies of the *Colorado Springs Summit,* all folded back to reveal the stories of Gregory Landis.

He glanced through the stack. "You're Landis?" he asked, amazed.

"Have been for the past five years." She sat across from him, peering at his face to catch his reaction.

He wasn't sure if his response was obvious to her or not. He felt awed and impressed. Writing stories for the newspaper? She had more grit to her than he'd imagined.

He smiled, and her answering smile formed a warm arc between them, an invisible rainbow that held them and moved them and molded them until they forgot all else.

The spell lasted until Vessel's measured tread sounded over their heads.

"We'd best get back upstairs," Penny said, her cheeks delightfully pink. "You've still got to fulfill your end of the bargain, you know." Scooping up the bundle, she locked the newspapers back into the cabinet.

"Would you like to join the game of Parchessi?" Justin asked as they walked together down the hall. "It's great fun."

"If you want," she replied. Then after a small pause, "On the other hand, I think I'd rather sit in the parlor. It's been a long day, and I'm a little tired. Maybe tomorrow we can play."

"In that case, let's find a lamp and take a look at the sketchbooks. I brought both of them, so we could be awhile."

When they reached the parlor, the men were already in positions on opposite sides of the table, generals surveying their territory. Vessel was in his glory.

Sitting close together on the sofa with a lighted gas lamp on the wall behind them, Justin opened the satchel and drew out two wide weathered books. Their paper covers were wrinkled and smudged with charcoal.

He hesitated, running his hand over the top cover. "I have one favor to ask of you before we begin."

"Yes?" She turned to him expectantly and the light played across the smooth curve of her cheek.

"Be honest," he said, gently. "I want your true and unvarnished opinion. Agreed?"

"Of course." She smiled, and he thought his heart would stop.

Forcing himself to get to the matter at hand, he opened the book and moved it over so the binding fell between them, and they each held one side.

He kept turning pages at slow intervals. He'd expected to feel embarrassed or nervous, but instead he was at peace. She was a kindred spirit in the arts, something he'd never found before.

Suddenly her hand flew out to stop him from turning the page. Before them lay two kittens in the midst of a rough and tumble, a knot of legs and tails done in charcoal.

She didn't speak for a full minute, her expression intent as she studied the details. "This is marvelous," she murmured, glancing at him. "One is a calico and the other a tiger. How did you do that?"

"We had cats in the stable," he replied. "I loved to watch them play. These two scrappers were always going at it. One day I took my charcoals out and captured them." He gazed at the picture and pointed to the bottom right edge of the image. "I hide my name and the date within the picture itself. See here?" He checked the date and calculated. "I was twelve when I did this one."

"You did this when you were twelve?" she gasped. "I can't believe that. You have talent, Justin," she declared. "You must pursue this." She turned the page, eager now to see what lay ahead.

They spent the next two hours with the sketchbooks while the men exclaimed and complained over their game. Justin wanted the evening to last forever.

"Will you come back for Christmas breakfast with us?" she asked as they neared the end of the last volume.

"I don't want to intrude on your family time," he said, though he wanted it in the worst way.

"We'd love to have you and Vessel come for the day tomorrow."

Her father let out a roar, and she chuckled, turning to watch them.

"Set back again!" Mr. Joshua cried. He settled himself into the chair. "Don't look for any quarter from this side," he declared. "You're not getting any."

Vessel laughed. "Nor you from me, I promise you." He shook the dice in their little black cup and poured them onto the board. "Five!"

"They're overgrown children," Penny said, still laughing.

"Warriors," Justin corrected. "There's a difference."

She tilted her head as an idea struck her. "You know, we should have a party tomorrow, invite some more people in and have a good time."

She counted on her fingers. "I'll have Farley bring Diane. He'll be delighted at that, believe me. I'll invite Margaret and Catherine, friends of mine from our church." She ticked them off. "You and Vessel." She turned to him. "Do you have any friends from the hotel that you'd like to bring along?"

Justin drew up. He'd like to bring Teddy in the worst way. What could be more heartless than to leave a good friend alone on Christmas while he himself was having a high old time? But could he trust Teddy to keep mum?

"What is it, Justin?" she asked. "You look worried."

He smiled. "Nothing could be wrong tonight," he murmured, leaning a little closer. "I was just thinking about who I could invite."

"You don't have to tell me now," she said, looking down at her six extended fingers. "You could bring two friends, and we'd still have room for everyone." She laughed again. "Or bring more, and we'll move down into the restaurant."

He laughed. "I'll remember that."

The lock rattled, and Farley kicked the

outer door open. A blast of cold air brought Penny to her feet to see what her brother was doing. Justin came along behind her.

Farley had his back to them. He yanked hard on something out of sight, and a snowy Christmas tree slid into the hall.

"Oh, look at the wet!" Penny cried and ran to get some rags to wipe up the floor.

Farley pulled the tree in far enough to get around it in the narrow hall, then hurried to fetch a bucket from the stoop and close the door. "Where do you want this?" he asked when Penny returned.

"In the parlor alcove," she said, "but not until it's drier. Oh, why didn't you bring it in *before* it started snowing."

Testily, he replied, "If I'd known it was going to snow, I would have."

She let out a frustrated gasp. "Oh well, there's no hope for it now. I'll put towels on the floor under it until it drips dry." She turned toward the galley kitchen. "We'll have to move the furniture to make way."

Farley took off his damp cap and coat and hung them up. He glanced at Justin. "Let's get that sofa moved and those two small tables."

The men set to work while Penny removed the hurricane lamp to her bedroom for safekeeping. Farley carried the bucket of sand to the alcove, and the men set the tree upright in it then filled it almost full of water. Penny quickly set towels on the wooden floor beneath it.

"It's beautiful even without any ornaments," she said as she smiled at Justin. "I guess we'd best get busy. I made popcorn to string up and some paper ornaments to put together."

"Candles?" Farley asked her.

"A dozen of them," she said then went on, "We're having a party here tomorrow afternoon at two o'clock. I'd like you to invite Diane, Catherine, and Margaret." She glanced at him. "You are going out in the morning, aren't you?"

He nodded. "I'm supposed to be at Diane's house around ten o'clock. I'll stop in to see the others on my way by." He flexed his shoulders and stretched his back. "I put a crick in my back pulling that thing up the stairs." He rotated one shoulder and then the other. Glancing at Penny, he asked, "So, what have you got planned for the party? Parlor games? Food?"

"Both!" she announced. "We've got plenty of cake left in the ice box. I'll make coffee, and we'll be set."

"Sounds like a great time," he said, pleased. "Now, where are the candles?"

"In the kitchen." She hurried to find them along with some strong thread and two needles. When she returned, she gave Farley the box of candles, then handed Justin a needle and a long length of thread. She placed a bowl of popcorn between her and Justin on the sofa.

Mr. Joshua whooped over some play in the game, and Farley headed over to see what was happening. In a few moments, he returned and they worked at decorating the tree for the next hour.

When his job was finished, Farley lifted the curtain and peered into the night. "It's really starting to come down out there."

"Is it?" Penny stopped sewing a paper ornament and joined him at the window. "I love to watch it snow."

Justin joined Penny at the window. Thick snowflakes swirled around the street lamps.

"We'd best get started home," he said, noticing a thin coating of white on the ground. "I hope this doesn't keep us away tomorrow."

"So do I," she murmured, gazing shyly up at him.

At that moment, Vessel cried, "That's it! Game point. You win this round, old man."

Farley stepped to the table. "I'd like to get in on the game tomorrow," he said.

"Tomorrow?" his father asked, a hearty note in his voice.

"Penny's got a party planned for the afternoon," Farley told him.

Penny added, "I've invited them to come for breakfast and stay for the day," she said.

"Excellent!" Mr. Joshua said. His round cheeks almost hid his eyes when he smiled.

Slipping the colored playing pieces into a small velvet pouch, Vessel said, "I'll leave the game here, if it's all right with you, Michael."

"Good idea," Justin put in. "It's snowing, and you'd get the box wet carrying it home."

Vessel became concerned. "Snowing? We'd best be going then." He flipped the board closed with a quick movement and had the box top in place within seconds.

Justin returned to their coats hanging in the hall. Penny followed him. "Maybe you'd better leave the suit here tonight," she said. "It'll get wet if you take it now."

"I'll leave the sketchbooks here, too," he told her. "No sense taking any chances with them either."

"Of course. I'll put them away in my room."

Vessel trundled into the hallway, and Penny moved to give him room to put on his coat.

"Thank you both for coming," she said warmly.

"Yes, thanks for coming," Mr. Joshua said, standing at the end of the hall. "I don't know when I've had such a good time."

The men shook hands all around and said their good nights. Justin clasped Penny's hand in his for a lingering moment. He had a difficult time pulling himself away from her.

"Tomorrow!" he whispered as he left her.

Her answering smile made his heart sing. "Ten o'clock," she said.

Carefully moving down the snowy stairs, Justin and Vessel hurried down the street, anxious to get out of the bitter cold and the biting wind.

"I owe you an apology," Vessel said when they paused at a street crossing.

"We differ on that," Justin said. "I should be apologizing. I put you in a difficult position tonight."

"Not at all. It was jolly good fun," he replied, stepping into the street. "What a marvelous family." He chuckled. "What a delightful young lady, Justin my boy."

Justin nodded, and his stomach turned into a leaden knot. What would she think of him when she learned who he really was? When she learned that he hadn't been honest with her?

Penny turned out the gaslights as she made her way to her room. Farley and Daddy had already turned in. It was close to midnight, and they were all exhausted.

She paused in the doorway to her room, leaning against the doorjamb with her head resting on the smooth woodwork. What a wonderful man Justin was. She'd never met anyone like him . . . and she probably never would again. He was sweet and thoughtful, kind and generous, talented . . . and a dedicated Christian. And so handsome with those brown eyes and that cute little dimple in his chin.

She sighed and pulled her door gently closed. She'd had a few crushes in her life, but never one steady beau. A couple of years ago, she would have been bouncing with excitement after spending the evening with an attractive gentleman, but tonight was different. Tonight, she felt a calm warmth deep within her. She wanted to hug it to herself and never let it go.

Slowly changing into her flannel night-gown, she turned out the last light, snuggled under the goose-down comforter, and soon fell into a deep sleep.

CHAPTER 8

When Justin and Vessel arrived at the penthouse, Teddy came out of his room dressed in a thick blue robe and wearing slippers. His straw-like hair was tousled, and he looked like he was ten years old.

"Good morning," he said with a sleepy grin.

"Good night, Master Teddy," Vessel said and went straight to his quarters.

"Did you get any rest?" Justin asked, taking off his coat. He laid it over the arm of a nearby chair.

"About three hours," Teddy replied with a wide yawn. He rubbed his eyes. "I woke up a few minutes ago, starving." He gazed around the dining room. "Do you have a kitchen hereabouts?"

Justin shook his head. "Sorry. But I do have a loaf of bread and a piece of hard cheese. Vessel keeps some in a cupboard for an emergency."

"Well, I'd call this one," Teddy replied, rubbing his stomach. "I ate a big dinner. Can't imagine why I'm so famished."

Justin lit a lamp in the dining room and opened a cupboard door. "I'll bet you haven't eaten much the last day or so. Too wrought up."

The other man nodded. "You've pegged that right. Alice had me jumping through hoops. It wasn't pleasant, and that's a fact."

Justin set the food on the table and poured them both water from a carafe. "I'm glad you're up," he said, sitting across from Teddy at the table. He waited for his friend to cut a slab of cheese and chew for a moment before saying, "I'm in a sticky situation, Ted, and I'm going to have to call in a couple of favors."

Teddy stopped chewing. "You don't say," he said around his mouthful.

Justin started with the restaurant fiasco and Penny's mistaking him for a waiter. "She gave me fifty cents to get a haircut," he said ruefully.

Teddy's eyes grew round. "You are pulling my leg, Justin Van der Meer. You surely are."

"I am not!" he declared. "You can ask Vessel in the morning. He knows about this, too."

Teddy's expression became intent. "And

you took it?"

Justin nodded. "I got the haircut, too."

Teddy pulled his left earlobe. "Okay, okay." He held up his hand to stop Justin's storytelling. "Let's go back for just a minute. You've left out a vital detail."

"What?"

"What does she look like?" he demanded.

"Penny?" Justin gazed into the yellow light reflected in the table's glossy top. "The top of her head comes up to here." He held his hand level at a point below his shoulder. "She has delicate features and the bluest eyes I've ever seen. Her hair is so blond it almost glows. She wears it up —" He had his hand over the top of his head then froze when he caught sight of Teddy's sardonic smile. Ignoring it, he went on, "She's spunky and smart . . ."

"Got it bad, I see," Teddy said, chuckling. He took another bite of bread and cheese.

"I've never met anyone like her," Justin said. Suddenly, he grew serious. "She still doesn't know who I am, Teddy. And she can't find out yet. You've got to help me keep it mum."

"Keep talking," he said, still chewing.

"We're invited to her house for Christmas Day. I want to take you along, but you have to promise me you'll watch what you say.

Promise you won't give me away."

"That's a hard promise to make, Justin," Teddy said. "What if I slip up?"

"So far it hasn't been hard to avoid certain topics. When she asks something personal, I change the subject or make a comment that has nothing to do with what she asked. She hasn't seemed to notice."

"All I can promise is that I'll do my best." He squinted at Justin. "How many times have you seen this girl?"

Justin told of their two practice sessions and Christmas Eve at the Joshuas' apartment, leaving out the part about his sketches and her writing. "We're all invited back for Christmas breakfast at ten in the morning," he finished. "You, me, and Vessel."

Teddy wrapped the remaining food into its paper container and pushed it toward Justin. "When's this meeting again?"

"The day after tomorrow. We'll spend tomorrow with the Joshua family, and then the next day I've got to get through that meeting." He rubbed the stubbly hair on the back of his head and tried to smooth it down. "Penny's going to be there watching my every move. And boy is she tough to please."

Teddy yawned again.

Justin picked up the small bundle of food.

"We've got to get to bed, or we'll meet ourselves getting up. It's close to two a.m."

"Tomorrow I may prop myself in a corner somewhere and sleep," Teddy said. "I'm bone weary."

"You could come later," Justin told him, relieved at the thought. "If you want to sleep in, I'll leave directions on the table here so you can find your way when you're ready." The less time Teddy spent with Penny the better.

"We'll see how I feel in the morning," he said, shuffling toward the hall. "Merry Christmas," he mumbled and gave a little salute as he disappeared into his room and closed the door.

Justin took his time putting away the food and turning out the lights. Tonight in Penny's parlor he'd had a feeling of living in a world that wasn't real. The Joshua family lived a quiet, simple life. Their lot was hard in some ways, sure. But so was his. So was everyone's, when it came down to it. The problems were different, but they were still problems.

He changed his clothes and slid into bed. Did he dare to dream that Penny would someday live in his world? Would she want to?

He turned over and closed his eyes. *You*

can stop dreaming, you big dolt, he thought. *Once she finds out that you've been holding back on her, she'll be so disgusted with you that she'll probably refuse to see you again.*

An ache swelled in his chest, and he shoved the thought aside. It was too painful to dwell on, even for a minute.

No one in the Joshua house stirred until nearly nine o'clock. Christmas was the one day of the year when they had nothing to do. The restaurant was closed every Sunday, but there were church services to prepare for, so a day of complete rest was extremely rare.

Farley was combed and dressed when Penny first ventured from her room. She wore a robe and her hair hung about her shoulders.

Farley kissed her cheek. "Merry Christmas, sis," he said.

She gave him a soft smile. "Merry Christmas." She looked at his starched shirt. "Are you going so soon?"

"If I'm going to stop in on Margaret and Catherine, I'll have to leave in a few minutes."

"Wait! I've got presents." She hesitated. "I hate to wake up Daddy."

"Don't. The presents will keep until I get

back. I should be here around noon. After breakfast, Diane's folks are going to visit her grandmother. It's a family time, and I'm going to bow out."

"That will be fine," she said, relieved. "Justin will be here in an hour, and I still need to dress."

"He's a nice fellow," Farley said, giving her a wry smile.

She beamed. "I noticed."

He kissed her cheek again. "I hope it works out for you. He's a nice guy."

Her cheeks felt warm.

Farley glanced at the mantel clock and hurried away, leaving Penny to her primping.

Justin started the day by washing up to clear the fuzz from his brain. He shouldn't have stayed up so late talking to Teddy. Now he was paying for it.

Half an hour later, he and Vessel left the penthouse as quietly as they could so Teddy could catch up on his sleep. Justin pulled the door closed behind him with a feeling of intense relief. He'd left directions and a hand-drawn map on the table. With any luck, Teddy would sleep until two p.m. It wasn't unheard of.

Justin carried a small bundle under his

arm. As was the family custom, he'd given Vessel a generous cash gift that morning. Arrangements had been made last fall for every servant in every one of Justin's homes to receive something as well, from parlor maid to stable boy. The Van der Meers were frugal but definitely not cheap.

The snow had stopped during the night, leaving the town with a clean-washed feeling. Mercifully, the wind had died down. The air was crisp, and the snowy sidewalks crunched beneath their shoes.

Justin drew in a cleansing breath and energy flowed through him. In five more minutes he'd be with Penny.

When they reached the stairs, they were already swept clean. Penny opened the door before they had a chance to knock.

"Merry Christmas!" she cried, stepping back to let them in. "You must be frozen. Come in where it's warm." She wore a dress of soft brown fabric with a hint of red in the color.

Justin laid his bundle on the bench beneath the coat hooks and took off his coat.

"Farley has already gone to Diane's house," she said. "He'll be back in a couple of hours." She beamed at Vessel. "Daddy's in the kitchen downstairs. He'll be up soon with our breakfast tray."

"It must be strange having a father who cooks," Justin said, following her into the dining room. The table was set for six.

"Not to me." She let out a small, enchanting laugh. "He's been cooking all my life."

Mildly embarrassed, Justin showed her the bundle. "I brought a gift — a thank-you for having us over."

"Justin, you shouldn't have gone to any trouble," she said, eyeing the rolled-up cloth. "Why don't you leave it by the Christmas tree? Farley went out before Daddy was up, so we haven't exchanged our gifts yet. We can do it all at once." She smiled. "Thank you for being so thoughtful."

He swallowed and tried to fight back the heat crawling up his neck and into his cheeks — a lost cause.

A booming voice brought Vessel to the door of the inside stairs, and Michael Joshua stepped in carrying a tray wider than his girth. It was loaded with scrambled eggs, sausage, bacon, golden biscuits, and a stack of pancakes eight inches high. "Coffee's still in the kitchen," he said. "And there's another tray with the butter and syrup for these hotcakes." He set the entire tray in the middle of the table.

Penny headed for the stairs with Justin at her heels. Oh, the glory of a chance to speak to her alone.

"Does he always go all out for Christmas breakfast?" he asked her when they reached the bottom.

"This year is special," she said, gazing up at him. "He feels it, too." A hint of sadness touched her smile. "You've been good for us," she said. "Even for Daddy. You've made us look ahead instead of behind."

He thought about that for a moment. "So have you," he said. "I'm afraid I was caught in the same trap." She reached for the tray, and he had to fight back the urge to stop her and take her in his arms.

Lifting the coffeepot with a potholder lying beside the stove, he caught up to her on the fourth step. "Be careful you don't trip," he said.

She sounded a little breathy when she said, "I'm used to these stairs, Justin." She laughed then said, "Don't worry. I won't fall on you."

"It's that open pitcher of syrup I'm worried about," he retorted.

She was still laughing when she stepped into the dining room.

They took their places at the table, and Mr. Joshua offered thanks.

Reaching for the nearest dish, piled high with bacon and sausage, Vessel said, "When

I was a boy in England, we'd always look forward to having Crackers beside our plates at Christmas breakfast."

"Crackers?" Penny asked, wrinkling her dainty nose. "For breakfast?"

He chuckled. "They were party favors, my dear," he said, "a fascinating invention." He forked meat onto his plate and passed the platter to Justin beside him. "They were about this long." He held his hands about eight inches apart. "A tube shape decorated with brightly colored paper. Each end held a string or a loop, so two people could pull each end, like a wishbone. When the middle gave way, it made a great cracking sound and some kind of treat would fall out. Whoever got the biggest half kept the treat."

"Candy?" Mr. Joshua asked.

"Sometimes. But it could be a small toy or a gaudy hat made of tissue paper." Vessel smiled at the memory. "We used to wear those hats and run about like little hooligans until Mother would have enough of it and set us down with a picture book or some such." He sighed. "Wonderful days."

Penny said, "Mother always gave us something she'd made with her own hands — a scarf, some gloves, a sweater . . . sometimes a dress or a coat."

A warm silence gave them a moment to

enjoy the food. When they finished, Penny said, "Daddy, would you mind if we read the Christmas story from the Bible before we leave the table?"

"Not at all," he said. "I'd enjoy that. I haven't heard it for years."

She hurried to her room and brought back a thick book with a worn black cover. "This was Mother's," she said. She handed it to Justin. "Would you mind reading for us?"

He opened the yellowed pages and began to read, " 'And it came to pass in those days, that there went out a decree from Caesar Augustus that all the world should be taxed . . .' " He read slowly and with feeling for the next five minutes. Then he gently closed the book.

"That was beautiful," Penny breathed. "I can never listen to that story without being touched."

Mr. Joshua cleared his throat. "Would you like to move into the parlor?" he asked. "We can take our coffee in there." He glanced at Penny. "We'll clear this up later. There's plenty of time today."

They had scarcely sat down when Farley burst in, stamping snow from his boots and grinning widely. "It's a gorgeous day," he said. His cheeks were red and his nose, too.

Penny laughed at him. "You look half

frozen. What are you talking about?"

Leaving his boots in the hall, he dropped his coat over its peg and padded into the parlor in his stocking feet. "It's sunny, very little breeze. The snow is sparkling."

She slanted a look at him and gave him a sly grin. "Sounds romantic."

He let out a loud laugh but didn't comment on that. Instead he said, "For your information, both Margaret and Catherine are coming over this afternoon. And . . ." He hesitated to give his announcement a build up, "Catherine's father is going to hitch their sleigh for us after dark. The streets are covered with snow, perfect for a ride."

Penny let out a delighted gasp. "That's wonderful!" She looked at Justin. "Can you stay for that? You won't have to work early in the morning, will you?"

He grinned. "I can stay. I wouldn't miss it for anything."

Farley pulled a chair from the dining table, placed it next to the Christmas tree, and sat down.

"Now that you're here," his father told him, "we can exchange our gifts." He spoke to Vessel. "I hope you don't mind. We didn't have time to do this earlier today."

"By all means," Vessel said.

113

Wrapped in brown paper and tied with string, or bundled in brightly colored cloth, the gifts were distributed and quickly opened.

When the Joshua family had finished their exchange, Justin reached for his own bundle. He felt awkward. "I brought this as a thank-you for your hospitality," he said, handing it to Penny.

With a wondering glance at him, she unwrapped it and gasped with pleasure. Inside lay a small wooden box, carved roses covering the sides and lid.

"How lovely!" she exclaimed.

"It's something that's been in our family for a while," he told her. "I thought you might like it."

"I love it!" She turned it one way and then the other, admiring the workmanship. "Thank you, Justin!" Her sparkling eyes made him want to shout or dance or sing. Or all three.

He had to limit himself to a softly spoken, "You're quite welcome, Penny."

"And now, let's set up a game of Parchessi," Mr. Joshua said.

"How many can play?" Penny asked. She carefully set the box on a small table near her chair and stood up.

"Only four," her father said. "One at each

114

corner of the board."

"In that case, Justin and I will clear the food away, Daddy," she said, looking at Justin for confirmation. "Would you mind sitting out this time?" she asked him.

"Not at all," Justin said, eager to help. He'd wash dishes for six hours straight if it meant five minutes alone in the kitchen with Penny.

CHAPTER 9

Farley picked up the wide tray and loaded it with dishes. "I'll carry this one. You get the plates," he said. "Go ahead and start without me," he told his father. "I'll get in on the second round."

To Justin's chagrin, Farley seemed to be planning to stick with them until the job was finished.

Scraping food into small dishes to put into the icebox, Farley said, "Don't you think Justin has vastly improved, Penny? I don't think he needs any more practice at all."

Wiping a cup, Justin waited for her reply.

"You're right. No more practice." She flicked a small bit of suds at Farley. "Who wants to practice on Christmas Day anyway?"

Farley dodged the suds. "You don't want to open that can of worms, sis," he warned.

She laughed. "Who said I don't?"

He pointed to the clock. "Diane will be

here in half an hour."

"Spoilsport." She dug into the dishpan for another plate and the dishes began to fly as they finished cleaning up. Ten minutes later, Penny set the cider on the back of the stove to simmer.

Mr. Joshua and Vessel had the Parchessi game set up when the young people returned. Farley joined the men while Justin and Penny sat in the parlor. Minutes flew by, and Justin wished that for the second time in history the sun would stand still.

In the middle of the second game, a light tapping at the door brought Farley to his feet. "That's Diane!" he said, moving to the hall. "She's got the girls with her," he called back to the dining room two seconds later, then swung open the door.

Giggles and gasps filled the hallway. Penny left the parlor to join her friends and soon returned with them. "This is Catherine Bagley," she said with a small wave at the dark-haired girl. Three inches taller than Penny, Catherine had a regal bearing, yet a sincere and friendly smile as she said hello.

"Margaret Meadows," Penny said, beaming at the second girl. Smaller and slighter, she had a boyish smile and hair the color of honey. She wore a yellow dress with a large orange scarf tied about her shoulders.

Farley appeared behind them with his arm around a third girl, an olive-skinned beauty. "And Diane Wallace." He winked at her. "Soon to be Joshua."

Her blush gave her a radiant glow.

Farley looked at the Parchessi board. "Sorry to bow out, but I'm part of the entertainment committee." He stretched to remove his pieces from play.

"Well, Entertainment Committee," Catherine said, "what are we going to do?"

At that moment, another tap sounded on the door. Farley looked at Penny. "Who else is coming?" he asked.

"Teddy!" Justin exclaimed, remembering him for the first time that morning. "A friend of mine. I'd forgotten all about him."

Penny let the young man in, and he joined the group. Justin made the introductions, then he and Farley moved still more chairs into the parlor so that the seven of them sat in a circle along the walls of the tiny room.

"Charades!" Penny announced, clapping her hands. She grinned at Justin. "We've quite a few people here who are strangers. This way we'll get to know each other."

Justin stiffened. He had never been comfortable playacting. Teddy sent him a wide grin and hooked one arm over the back of his chair. He'd been a thespian at Berkeley

118

and thoroughly enjoyed Justin's discomfort.

"Do you have a list of items?" Farley asked.

Penny drew a folded page from her dress pocket and waved it in the air. "I'll have to be the moderator because I already know what they are." She surveyed the group. Catherine wore an amused half-smile, and Diane chewed her bottom lip.

Penny stood. "Would you mind trading chairs with me, Margaret? That way I'll be in the center. Each side of the room is a team."

"Of course," Margaret said and quickly moved into Penny's chair, which put Margaret between Teddy and Justin. Teddy straightened in his chair and pulled his arms in a little. Margaret licked her lips.

"Farley's team starts," Penny announced. "Who's going to be first?"

Catherine stepped forward. Penny folded the paper back so only the top line was visible, then showed it to her.

Catherine shrugged and quirked in one side of her mouth. She faced Farley and Diane, pointed from one of them to the other, and then touched the fourth finger of her left hand.

"Married!" Farley burst out.

Catherine shook her head and tugged at

her finger again.

"Engaged!" Diane cried.

"Point," Penny said. She turned to the other team.

"You go," Justin told Teddy. "You're a lot better at this than I am."

Teddy rubbed his palms on his pants legs as he stood. When he got the word, he grinned. Whirling, he pointed directly at Justin's midsection.

"Chest!" Justin said.

Teddy shook his head and pointed again, this time at Justin's head.

Margaret guessed "hair," "face," and "eyes," but got nowhere.

Justin tried "man," "boy," "American," "friend," and finally "handsome" as a parting joke, then gave up. "What was it?" he demanded.

Teddy shook his head, disgusted. "Wealthy. What else?"

Penny looked worried and sent a suspicious glance toward Justin, then asked Teddy, "Why would you point to Justin for that word?"

Justin glared at Teddy, and his friend's freckled face quickly turned the color of a ripe tomato. He covered his mouth with his palm and pulled his jaw downward. "I'm sorry," he said, letting his hand drop. "I did a bad job on that one." He turned to Penny. "Am I disqualified?"

She glanced at Farley. "Can we give them another try?" she asked. "I think that was a mix up."

Farley nodded. "Beginner's grace," he said.

Relief in the slope of his shoulders and angle of his chin, Teddy came to Penny for another word. "I apologize," he said. "I'll get the right of it this time."

They played for the next hour with Teddy on his best behavior. Farley's team won the final point by guessing "signature" when Diane pretended to hand herself a bill and then she scribbled on the bottom of it with her finger.

"Anyone for spiced cider?" Penny asked as they broke up. "I have some in the kitchen downstairs."

Justin lingered toward the back of the group when the others filed out, expecting Teddy to naturally join him. When the young men had a brief moment on the stairs out of earshot of the others, Justin whispered. "You just cost me a year of my life, pal."

"I'm so sorry," Teddy said, shaking his head at his own stupidity. "I lost my mind for a few seconds. That's all I can say."

Justin clapped him on the back. "No harm done, but let that be a lesson for you. Watch it!"

Teddy nodded then grinned. "She's special," he whispered. "I can see why you're worried." He picked up speed and joined Catherine at the bottom of the stairs.

Continuing at a slower pace to give himself time to settle his mind, Justin arrived at the kitchen door as steaming mugs were passed around. They moved into the dining room and pushed two tables together so everyone could sit together.

While the rest were occupied, Penny drew near to Justin and whispered, irritated, "Did you tell Teddy about our arrangement?"

He felt a shock go through him.

Her eyes were wide and probing. "Why did he point at you for the word 'wealthy' if you hadn't?" Her lips tightened. "You shouldn't have done it, Justin. It could ruin everything."

Unable to defend himself, Justin didn't reply. She turned her back to him and joined the others, sitting near the opposite end of the table, far away from him.

Farley said, "This is great cider, sis."

Murmurs of approval went through the group.

Still looking disgruntled, she sipped from

her mug and didn't reply.

"How about playing Twirling the Trencher?" Catherine asked. "That would be fun."

"Oh, no," Farley said. "Remember what happened last time we played that."

The girls giggled and looked at each other.

"Who wants to play?" Catherine asked. She raised her hand, and the rest of the girls followed her lead. None of the men moved.

"It's four to three," she announced.

"We can stand in front of the kitchen doors," Penny said. She dashed into the kitchen and soon returned with a brown wooden tray they used for carrying clean dishes to the drying racks.

The young people arranged themselves in a circle.

"I'll start." Catherine said, moving to the center of the ring. As Penny handed the tray to her, Catherine told her, "You can't have all the fun," and gave her a queenly smile.

Leaning over, she balanced the tray on one rounded corner and gave it a quick spin. It wobbled around. Catherine called out, "Teddy!" and stepped back.

Teddy lunged for it but the tray fell flat before he touched it.

"Forfeit!" the gang called. Every eye sought Catherine to see what punishment she'd mete out.

Teddy stood with his chin tucked in, a doubtful expression on his face, watching his tormenter.

Catherine said, "What was the name of your worst girlfriend and why?"

He shoved his hands into his pockets and grinned. "I don't mind telling that one," he said. "It was Alice. She dumped me on Christmas Eve — with no warning."

Diane and Margaret looked sympathetic.

Catherine lowered her dark lashes and smiled at him. "Now it's your turn," she said.

Teddy gave the tray a spin. It stood upright, a brown, fat blur. "Farley!" he cried.

Farley dove into the center and caught the tray before it toppled over. Holding it in one hand, he looked triumphant and grinned at Diane. He gave it a spin and called, "Justin!"

Caught off guard, Justin dashed into the center, overshot, and collided with Farley. The tray landed at his feet.

Farley took his time, savoring the moment, then he asked Justin, "What was the name of your last girlfriend?"

Teddy gasped and started to laugh. His face turned the color of an old brick.

Sending a warning look toward his erstwhile friend, Justin was actually glad for Teddy's distraction. His last girlfriend was Louisa Morgan, eldest daughter of J. P. himself, the famous tycoon. There was no way he could utter her name. Every girl in the room would immediately know who she was.

He lifted his chin and sent a last sharp glance at Teddy, who was still chuckling and coughing by spells, and said, "Double-forfeit."

Farley looked surprised. "Double-forfeit?"

Justin nodded and braced himself. A double forfeit meant drastic measures. He only hoped this penalty had nothing to do with his true identity. If he refused again, he could end up washing dishes for Farley for the next week.

Farley looked around as though finding inspiration for an extreme sentence. Focusing on Justin again he said, "Pick someone in this room to slap you in the face." He glanced at Penny. "And if they don't do a proper job of it, I'll pick someone else myself."

Justin took his time looking at each one. He felt like a kid sent out to cut his own switch. Grandma had pulled that one on him too many times. Bring back one that was too small, and she'd go out and find a tree limb to work him over, at least that's the way it seemed to him at the ripe old age of eight.

He looked at Teddy — all too eager. The twist of Catherine's shapely lips showed she would love to show off her audacity. Diane and Margaret would probably give him a little tap and have Farley bellowing, "Foul!"

He gazed at Penny and didn't like the intent expression on her face. But . . . all in all, she was his best bet. "Penny," he said.

Without giving him a chance to set himself, she marched up to him, swung, and connected with his cheek. He felt the reverberation to his toes. His head snapped sideways. An inferno blossomed in his cheek.

"Oh!" she cried, her lips forming an oval. "I'm so sorry! I didn't mean to hit you that hard." She reached out as though to touch his cheek. Instinctively, he drew back. "It's all red . . . my fingerprints. . . . You need a cold cloth." She turned as though to head toward the kitchen.

He lunged forward to catch her arm. "It's all right," he said. "Don't bother with that. It's all right."

She looked at him and winced. "It hurts me just to look at it." Turning, she glared at Farley. "That was mean, Farley Joshua. No more forfeits like that."

Farley laughed at her. "You're the one who hit him," he said.

Justin's head was reeling a little. Blinking once, he tried to shake it off.

Blushing to her roots, she returned to her place and stared at the floor. Teddy looked like he was about to pass out from a laugh attack.

"Your turn, old man," Farley told him.

To show he was a good sport, Justin quickly spun the tray and shouted, "Teddy!"

Still laughing, Teddy had hardly moved before the tray hit the floor. Justin's eyes narrowed. "Teddy, tell us the exact circumstances of how we first met," he said.

CHAPTER 10

Teddy's jaw dropped.

Locking eyes with him, Justin repeated the question, already sure what Teddy's answer would be.

"Double-forfeit!"

Grinning, Justin tilted his head back and said, "For your double-forfeit you must wear Margaret's scarf on your head and sing the Yum-Yum song, the finale from *The Mikado,* like the girls actually did it." Teddy had performed a major part in that play just a month before graduation. He had a terrific memory, and Justin was certain Teddy could remember the first few lines anyway.

"Aw, c'mon, Justin," Teddy complained. "You know I can't sing."

Catherine spoke up. "No whining, Teddy." She smiled provocatively. "We'd love to hear you. Wouldn't we, gang?"

Farley and Catherine clapped, and Diane joined them. Farley put two fingers in his mouth and whistled.

Penny pointed toward the swinging doors. "You can stand over there so we can all see you."

With a grimace and the loud sigh of a martyr, Teddy took the orange scarf from Margaret's outstretched hand. He flipped it over the top of his head and held the ends beneath his chin. He swayed side to side with the singsong of the rhyme and raced through the words in a shrill falsetto, "For he's gone and married Yum-Yum (Yum-Yum), Your anger pray bury, For all will be merry, I think you had better succumb (succumb) and join our expressions of glee!"

Catherine covered her face with her hands, fingers spread so she could still see him. Margaret turned red. She shook with laughter, tears streaming down her cheeks. Farley and Justin guffawed. The commotion was so loud they almost drowned out his last few words.

Whipping the scarf off, Teddy smoothed his hair with his free hand. As Teddy passed him, Justin clapped him on the back and said, "Good show!"

Handing the scarf back to Margaret, Teddy surveyed the group with a calculating eye, picking out the next victim before he spun the tray.

The game went on until the room grew dim and they had to stop to light some lamps. Justin got up to help Penny with them.

"Are Daddy and Vessel still playing that board game?" Penny asked Justin when the last lamp was glowing. After the slap, she'd seemed to forget her annoyance with him.

He shrugged. "More than likely. Vessel can play that game from dawn till midnight without any breaks. I've never seen anything like it. If he can't find an opponent, he'll play against himself."

"You're joshing," she said, chuckling. "They're two of a kind then. Daddy's always been that way about chess. At least he used to be before Mama died." She turned to the rest of the group and raised her voice. "Anybody hungry? I can bring out some leftovers."

"Sounds great," Farley said. "I'll help you." He put his arm around her shoulders and walked with her to the kitchen. Justin glanced at the table and noticed Teddy sitting next to Margaret. They seemed to be deep in conversation. So were Catherine and Diane.

Shoving his hands into his pockets, Justin strode to the kitchen doors and pushed inside. "Need some help?" he asked.

130

Penny looked up from a tray she was filling. "You can get the cheese. It's wrapped in cheesecloth in there." She nodded toward the pantry door.

He found the cheese and brought it back. As he returned, he caught sight of Farley's back disappearing through the doors.

"Still mad?" he asked Penny, sidling up to her at the table.

Her lips came out to form a thin ribbon. "Maybe." Taking the cheese bundle from him, she glanced at him. "Are you?"

He touched his cheek. It still burned a little. "I guess not. You were just playing the game."

"Something you need to learn to do," she replied archly. She cut ten slices of cheese in as many seconds, deftly arranged them, and handed him the tray. "You can carry that out. I'll bring a pitcher of water."

Wishing he could say more, Justin did as he was told. He figured it was better to run away and fight another day instead of trying to hash it out with her now. Tomorrow she'd understand everything . . . unfortunately.

The gang dug into the food like they hadn't eaten in two days. They were scarcely finished when a knock sounded at the dining room door.

"It's Daddy!" Catherine said.

Farley hurried to the door, and Mr. Bagley stepped inside. A small, thin man, he was completely covered except for a small slit for his eyes between his wool hat and his scarf.

"Have some hot coffee," Penny said when he approached the table. She looked at Farley. "I'm wondering if it's too cold for a sleigh ride," she said.

Farley replied, "We'll bundle up with blankets." He picked up a slice of cold ham and took a bite.

Pulling his scarf down, Mr. Bagley accepted the hot cup of steaming brew. "I'm much obliged, Penny," he said. He glanced at his daughter, Catherine, who stood two inches taller than he did. "We'll have to keep it short. That wind cuts like a knife. I'll run around the park and then head back." He looked at the plates in the young people's hands. "The horses are standing in the cold. We need to get moving."

Teddy gulped down the last of his dried apple pie, and Margaret set her plate on the table.

Penny turned to Justin. "Will you help me fetch everyone's wraps? They're in the upstairs hall."

Teddy said, "I'll go, Penny. You don't need to worry with that."

When they reached the stairwell, Teddy said, "Thanks for asking me over, man. That Margaret is a peach. A real honey."

Justin's brow lowered as he sent Teddy an unbelieving look. "I'm beginning to think that Alice wasn't so far off. If you could get interested in another girl that fast . . ." They reached the upstairs door, so he never finished the sentence.

Gathering two full armloads of coats, they headed back without any further conversation, and the group headed outside.

A large vehicle with double benches behind the driver, the sleigh was painted a glossy black with gold trim. Farley and Diane took the front seat. Then Margaret climbed in beside them, and Teddy leaped up after her. Catherine was already in the back, so Penny and Justin joined her.

Four thick rugs lay on each seat and four heated bricks wrapped in burlap were on the floor. It took a few minutes to get everyone wrapped and bundled, but they were finally ready to set off.

Mr. Bagley gave a shout and flapped the reins. The horses leaned into the weight and set the sleigh in motion. One black and one gray, their combined breath formed a wide steam cloud that trailed behind them, almost like a miniature locomotive. Frigid air blasted the faces of the young people. Penny wrapped her green-plaid scarf around her face. In a few moments, everyone else followed suit.

"Let's sing," Catherine said, her voice muffled.

Farley shook his head. "Let's not." He settled a little closer to Diane. "I don't feel like it right now. Can't we just have some peace for a few minutes?"

Justin was glad Farley had spoken up. With the brim of Penny's green felt hat brushing his cheek from time to time, the dark night, and a pale moon, singing was the last thing on Justin's mind.

If only this Christmas Day could last forever. He had the girl of his dreams close beside him with a soft smile on her lovely face and a gentle spark in her eyes whenever she looked at him. Even when she was irritated she was the sweetest, most attractive woman he'd ever met. Who needed a sloe-eyed debutante when an angel miraculously crossed one's path?

Tomorrow everything would change. She'd no longer need him to meet Mr. Gold Britches. At some point he would have to tell her the truth as well. From what he knew of Penny, when she found out who he really was, she would be furious and humiliated. Would she ever forgive him?

"Isn't the night beautiful?" she murmured.

He shifted so he could watch her from the corner of his eye. "Gorgeous."

"Are you ready for tomorrow, Justin?" she asked, her voice still soft and warm.

He stifled the urge to put his arm around her. "I'll never be ready," he said.

She sent him a questioning glance, and he went on, "After tomorrow I won't have any more excuses to see you. Do you think I could ever be ready for that?"

She beamed. "Must you have an excuse?"

His answering grin started at his heart and worked its way out. "I guess not," he said.

She moved a fraction of an inch closer.

He let out a silent groan. What was he going to do?

All too soon, they rounded the last curve in the park and crossed the exit. The sleigh jostled into the street and settled down with a soft hiss as it slid across the smooth pavement.

Ten minutes later, they reached the restaurant. The sleigh slowed, then stopped.

Mr. Bagley turned to look down at them. "I can take Catherine, Margaret, and Diane home now. It's too cold to walk."

From the slant of their shoulders and their sober expressions, none of them wanted to go. But practicality won out. Farley, Justin, and Penny stepped down. Teddy took a moment to say something to Margaret. She blushed and nodded. The next moment Teddy was on the ground, grinning. The four of them stood on the sidewalk and waved as the sleigh took off. The moment it turned the corner, they headed for the door.

"My feet are numb," Penny said. "Let's go into the kitchen. The stove probably still has some coals in it. We can make hot chocolate and sit close to the stove to drink it."

"Close enough to put our feet under it?" Teddy asked. He nudged Justin with his elbow. "A profitable evening," he said. "Thanks for the invitation." He turned to Penny with a deep nod. "And thanks to you, too."

She gazed at him, obviously trying to figure out what he was talking about. "You added a lot to the party, Teddy," she said with a teasing smile. "I've never seen *The Mikado,* but if that song is any indication of how funny it is, I'll save up for two years just to buy a ticket."

Teddy smirked. "Thanks . . . I think."

The warmth inside felt so good, but they still had a chill in their bones. Penny hurried to the kitchen to start the hot chocolate while the men cleared up the mess in the dining room. They stacked the few dishes beside the sink.

"I'll take care of the food while I'm waiting for this to get hot," Penny said, stirring a pan of milk on the stove.

Farley spoke to Teddy. "Let's see how the game's going upstairs."

"Great idea!" Teddy said. "Call us when the chocolate's ready."

They headed out the door and soon their heavy shoes thumped on the stairs.

Justin looked at the trays on the table. "What can I do to help?" he asked.

"How are you in the dishpan?" she asked.

"I've done my share," he replied, for the first time infinitely grateful that his dear grandmother had decreed he do kitchen chores. He rolled up his sleeves and turned on the hot water. "Do you have a boiler here?" he asked, watching the steam spiraling from the sink.

"The boiler heats the building and supplies the kitchen and bath with hot water. Daddy had it put in last year. Now I wonder how we ever lived without it."

He nodded. "I'm thinking of having one installed myself."

She looked surprised. "You are?"

"One of these days," he said, making a

show of placing silverware and mugs into the dishpan. He paused to ask, "What time should I arrive at the restaurant tomorrow?" He looked at her. "We are meeting there, aren't we?"

She nodded. "At fifteen past three at the Regal Astoria. Did I tell you that before?"

"I'll be there with bells on."

She loaded the tray with four white mugs and picked it up. "Don't get too far ahead of me with those dishes. I'll be right back."

The clock on the wall said nine o'clock. He was tired, and he knew Penny was. Maybe he should say good night when they finished clearing things up.

Penny came in laughing. "Daddy and Vessel have gotten those guys tied up in a game. Somehow they've figured out how to play teams — the old men against the youngsters. They're really going at it." She picked up a dishtowel. "I hung that suit in the hall, so you can pick it up on your way out. You'll need it tomorrow, you know."

"I was just thinking that we'd best head home."

"Already? It's only" — she glanced at the wall — "9:05."

"I don't want to wear out our welcome," he said.

She smiled at him. "You're not."

138

"Penny . . ." He tried to think of how to go on.

"Yes?"

"I just want to say that . . . no matter what happens tomorrow . . . the past two days have meant a lot to me."

"They've meant a lot to me, too, Justin." She set down the dish she was drying. "But you don't have to become a stranger when it's over. How would you like to come for dinner here tomorrow night at seven? We could talk about what happened with Mr. Matthews, whether our plan worked or not."

"Penny . . ."

"Are you trying to tell me something?" she asked. Her brow was crinkled, and she looked directly at him. "If you are, just tell me."

"There are things you don't know about me," he said. "My background and my past, things like that. When you find out, please don't make any hasty judgments. Can you promise me that?"

"Are you worried I'll think less of you because your family is poor?" she asked. "You don't have to worry about that, Justin. I don't care about those kinds of things."

Drying his hands he moved closer and smiled. "Try to hold on to that thought. I may ask you for it later."

"I'm glad you were the one in the dining room that day," she said. Her eyes were the color of forget-me-knots in May. Her face, so sweet and earnest.

He lowered his head and kissed her. She was precious, uncomplicated — everything he'd ever wanted in a woman.

"I have to tell you —" he said in a moment.

"Don't talk," she said, resting her cheek in the curve of his shoulder. "Everything's going be all right. You'll see."

CHAPTER 11

When Justin first awoke the next morning, the one thing he knew for certain was that everything was *not* going to be all right.

He was in love with Penny Joshua, hopelessly and helplessly in love with her. And he was a fraud, a big fat phony. At dinner tonight, he had to tell her everything. If she turned away, then he'd have to live with that. He couldn't sleep again before she knew.

Easing out of bed, he went into the bathroom to wash up.

He should have never agreed to the subterfuge. He could almost hear his grandmother's voice with her Dutch accent, "Vhat goes around, comes around." Well, things were surely going to come around like a bullwhip before nightfall.

He took his time dressing, then found Vessel in the dining room. For once the valet wasn't playing a game.

"Would you like me to call for breakfast, sir?" he asked.

"I'll have some cheese and bread with coffee," Justin told him. He noticed Teddy's open bedroom door. "Where's Teddy?"

Pouring them both a cup of coffee, Vessel said, "He went out at eight o'clock."

"In the morning? Where did he go?"

"I believe he had a date, sir. With Miss Margaret."

Justin laughed. "You're kidding me. Wow, that is rich." He sat at the table and sipped his coffee. Picking up a piece of bread, he carefully covered it with a slab of cheese and took a bite. "Things are getting out of hand," he said, swallowing. "What's going to happen when Margaret finds out who he is?"

Not a muscle of Vessel's face moved. "She'll be delighted, if I may say so. Her mother, too."

Justin moved his lips to one side. "You are so dry, Vessel. A real sober-sides."

Vessel's thin brows raised just a fraction. "Would you rather I tell you an untruth? I'm being perfectly frank."

Grinning in spite of himself, Justin said, "I only hope Penny will be delighted when she learns the truth about me. Somehow, I seriously doubt it."

"One never can tell, I'm sure."

Justin finished the last bite and stood. "You're a good friend, Vessel," he said. "Thank you for going with me yesterday. It was a great time."

He nodded. "A marvelous time, Master Justin. I won best out of five."

"Did you now? You and Teddy were going on so much about the game on the way home, I never got the final tallies."

"I'm to go over each Saturday afternoon while we're in town. The restaurant closes at three, you know. No dinner served on Saturday evening."

"Congratulations," he said. "I'd say you've finally met someone almost as intent as you are."

"Michael Joshua has a head on his shoulders, he has."

Justin took two steps toward his bedroom door. "I'm going to read awhile. The meeting is at three-thirty, too late for my liking. I want to get it over with."

"I've brushed that suit and hung it on the rack," Vessel said, clearing away the remains of breakfast. "I'm glad this is the last time you'll have to wear borrowed clothes. It's humiliating."

"I'm glad it's my last time, too, but for very different reasons," Justin retorted. He picked up his copy of *Ivanhoe* and found a soft chair. Whatever happened, at least everything would be over by tonight. At least he'd know one way or the other if he had a future with Penny Joshua.

When Penny had retired the night before, she'd expected to lie awake all night. Her mind was so full, her heart so overrun by wonder and excitement and pure joy. She had found *him*. And he was wonderful.

Father, she prayed, *thank You for being so good to me. . . .*

The next thing she knew, Daddy was pounding on her door. "It's six o'clock!" he bellowed then trudged away, his heavy footsteps shaking the planks on the floor.

She had to be in the dining room by seven. She rolled over and snuggled into her pillow for just one more moment, remembering Justin's smile, the look in his eyes when they were close together in the sleigh . . . that glorious kiss. How could she live for six whole hours until she saw him again?

Moaning, she threw back the covers and grabbed her thick robe. Shoving her feet into icy slippers, she shuffled into the single bathroom. When Daddy knocked at her door, it was his signal that he was finished and she could go in.

Half an hour later, she lingered in front of her bedroom mirror and smiled at her reflection. *Is this what love's like? I don't know what else it could be. It must be love.* Sighing, she tied on her apron and headed for the stairs.

Farley was finishing a plate of eggs and bacon when she arrived. "Nervous?" he asked.

"About what?"

"Our date with Montgomery!" he exclaimed. "Did you forget already?" He looked at her with narrowed eyes. "You look like the cat that swallowed the canary. What are you up to?"

"Up to?" She tried to look innocent. "Why, nothing. That is, the same thing you are. What do you think?"

"You look different." He peered at her. "It's Justin, isn't it?"

She felt her face grow warm.

He stood up and picked up his empty plate. "Be careful, Penny," he warned. "He's nice enough, but he has no family and no prospects. When you marry, you should move up. I'd hate to see you waiting tables for the rest of your life."

She reached up to kiss his cheek. "With you watching out for me, how can I go wrong?"

Justin arrived at the Astoria at precisely three fifteen. He felt tingly in his stomach, a feeling that had nothing to do with hunger. Ducking into the men's room to check his hair and straighten his tie, he drew in a calming breath and lifted his chin. Penny would be watching his every move. This must be his *magnum opus* when it came to etiquette.

The room had only three patrons when he arrived. He stood a moment in the doorway. Before him lay forty round tables covered in white with ten chandeliers hanging above them, glittering even at midday. Every empty table held four crystal goblets, an intricately folded lavender napkin inside each one.

As Justin scanned the room, Farley stood to show him where they were seated. His hair glossy with tonic, Farley was decked out in a gray suit and blue tie. He remained standing until Justin reached him.

"Have a seat," Farley said. "Mr. Montgomery hasn't arrived yet. He'll be here shortly."

Justin sat in the chair next to Penny. She wore a blue dress that made her eyes glow. "Hello," he said. "How are you today? I'm afraid we kept you too late last night."

"Not at all." Her cheeks turned a delicate shade of pink. "Anyway, the restaurant closes at three on Saturdays, so I won't have to work tonight."

"But you're having a guest for supper," he said, smiling.

She slowly blinked her eyes. "That's not work," she said.

"Here he comes," Farley whispered. "That's Mr. Montgomery in the black suit."

Justin drew up when he caught sight of the hotel owner. He was short and stocky with broad shoulders and meaty hands. He had a dark fringe of hair around a shiny dome top. The closer he came toward them, the more familiar he looked.

Trying unsuccessfully to keep from staring, Justin stood along with Farley as the newcomer arrived. Farley stuck out his hand. "Thank you for coming, Mr. Montgomery." He turned toward Justin. "May I introduce Justin —"

The older man boomed, "Van der Meer! Good to see you, son. My sympathies on the passing of your grandfather. Gustaf was a good man, the best."

Farley looked from Montgomery to Justin. "You know each other?"

Montgomery's fleshy cheeks curved in a

wide smile. "Why certainly. Justin Van der Meer, the new owner of the Nevada Salt Company. I've known his family for years."

Penny let out a small gasp. She covered her mouth with her hand. How could that be? He was a waiter. . . . She turned to look at his face, and his guilty eyes told her all she needed to know.

She fumbled for her purse. She'd never been so humiliated, so mortified in all her life.

Justin reached out to stop her, but she brushed his hand away. What kind of a game had he been playing with her? Whatever it was, it was cruel.

Without a word to anyone, she grabbed her coat and set off in a half-run toward the hotel lobby. She wanted to hide behind a closed door where no one could see her cry.

What a fool she'd been. Telling him about her writing, mooning over him like an idiot, letting him kiss her. He must have had a good hearty laugh when he got back to his hotel.

Tears blurred her vision, and she almost tripped on the hotel steps.

Justin stood paralyzed for ten seconds, then charged after her. He didn't catch her until they were on the hotel steps. She was sobbing and gasping for air, slapping at her face to brush the tears out of her eyes.

"Penny, stop! Please let me explain." His fingers found her forearm.

She pulled away from him. "Explain? That you've been making a fool of me the whole time? Laughing at me? Telling me lies and charming me into believing them?"

"I never told you a lie," he said, his voice quiet and serious. "Never once."

"But, you . . ." She found her handkerchief and pressed it to her nose.

"I didn't tell you the whole truth, Penny," he said. "That was wrong. I regretted it within twenty-four hours of meeting you. But by then it was too late to confess."

"Too late? Why too late?"

A small crowd had gathered on the steps to watch the drama. If Justin hated anything, he hated a scene. He put his arm about her shoulder. "Let's talk over here out of the way."

She followed him around the corner into an alley. They stopped behind a carriage, out of sight of the street.

"I'll tell you why it was too late," he said. "Because I was falling in love with you. I was afraid that if I told you who I really was, you'd run away from me." His lips twisted. "It seems I was right."

She didn't seem to hear him. "Why did you agree to help us in that ridiculous charade? Why would you want to?"

"I thought it was a lark," he said with an attempt at a smile. "Something fun. It is ironic, you know. And I've always loved a prank." He grew sober. "I never intended to hurt you or anyone else." He paused then went on. "There's more to the story than this. Can you hear me out?"

Sniffing and wiping her damp cheeks, she nodded.

"I came to Colorado Springs because I was sick of the holiday debauchery of the so-called upper class — the drinking, the immorality, the fake fun that really isn't fun at all. Besides that, half the mothers in the country have their scouts watching for me every time I come into a town so they can hound my every step to draw my attention to their daughters." He grimaced. "The *Times* calls me the most eligible bachelor of the decade."

He leaned down until they were almost nose-to-nose. "Do you know how that makes me feel? How could I ever trust a girl? How could I ever know that she wants me and not my money?"

He rubbed the back of his head and

smoothed it down. "I came here because I just had to get away from people and have quiet for a change. When I met you, I'd been here several days without a single thing to do besides read or play that game with Vessel. I was desperate for something to pass the time." His expression softened. "Then you came along."

"You deceived me. How can I forget that?"

"Penny, stop and think about what you just said. What were you planning to do to Mr. Montgomery? How is that different from what I did to you?"

She bent her head down and rubbed her forehead.

He pressed on. "You made an assumption, and I let it stand. That's exactly what you had planned for this meeting. Except for one difference. You *created* the situation for that purpose. I happened into it."

He clasped her by the shoulders. "I'm not condemning you, dear. I'm only asking you to forgive me. No, I'm begging you to forgive me. I love you, Penny. With all my heart I love you. Please don't send me away."

She looked up with deep questioning in her eyes. "You weren't laughing at me?" she asked.

"At the situation, not at you. Never at you."

"I suppose I have been rather foolish," she said. "I thought I was helping Farley, but all I did was make a big muddle of everything."

He drew her into his arms. "One thing you did not make a muddle of . . ." He lightly kissed her.

She leaned closer to him and put her arms around him. "What's that?"

"Us. If you hadn't gone off the deep end, we never would have met."

She smiled for the first time. "That's true, isn't it?"

"Sometimes God does let some good come out of our foolishness," he said. "Every once in a while, that is. And that leads me to my next point." He kissed her nose. "No more scheming after we're married. Promise?"

"Anything you say, dear Mr. Van der Meer," she replied with an arch look on her face.

He kissed her, and she clung to him. After all the hours of dreading his confession, Justin could hardly believe it was true. He closed his eyes and lost himself in the warmth of her embrace.

Penny's head was spinning. She melted in

152

Justin's arms. If only this moment could last forever.

Farley's voice brought her back to reality. Pulling away, she looked up to see Farley hurrying toward them. The carriage had moved away, and she hadn't even noticed.

"I've been searching all over for you," he said, a crestfallen look on his face. "Mr. Montgomery just left. He won't help me."

"Won't he?" Justin asked. His grin could have lit up a city block. "I guess that makes him the loser." He winked at Penny, and she leaned her cheek against his coat sleeve.

Putting his arm about her and holding her close to his side, Justin said to Farley, "Don't worry about that, old man. I'll wire my accountant right away. Will ten thousand be enough to get you started?"

Epilogue

267 Atlanta Blvd.
New York, New York
January 11, 1892

Dear Priscilla,

I hope this letter doesn't upset you too much, dear, but I just had to write to let you know the recent developments with Gustaf Van der Meer's grandson, Justin. He always seemed like such a nice boy, but he's shown a horrible lack of judgment once he inherited his grandfather's millions. Since you left for your tour of Europe, he has been a very busy man.

First (and worst of all) he married a poor girl with no family ties whatsoever, a nobody from start to finish. She's never come out into society, and from the looks of things, she never will.

Can you believe that? I know you had such hopes for your daughter, Veronica, when Justin visited New York again.

The newlyweds were married last month in the local church on the edge of town with only a few family members and close friends present. The wedding didn't even make the social column of the *Post.* The only reason I heard about it was that Madge Jefferson was in Colorado Springs at the time, and she told me while she was here for a Christmas party.

It seems Justin has built a house in Colorado Springs, a very tiny place with only ten rooms. Not only that, but the bride and groom intend to make it their principal residence. They've only three servants: a cook, a housekeeper, and a valet.

I don't know how in the world they will manage. I think the boy has lost his mind. You know his mansions in Nevada and Wisconsin are so elegant. Much more fitting for a man of his means.

Well, I must get this in the mail, Priscilla. The postman is due within the half hour. I hope you are having a grand time in France. Please send me a letter soon with all the details about what they are wearing this year. And tell Veronica she'll have to look elsewhere for an eligible bachelor.

(Think of all those millions gone to waste!)
With all my love,
I remain your sister,
Gladys Rothschild

Dear Reader,

Although I was raised in an Amish/
Mennonite family, my parents divorced
when I was thirteen. Deeply wounded by
an abusive stepfather, I was extremely shy.
Through a series of very painful events, I
was cut off from my parents for five years.
As God healed my wounded heart, my true
personality slowly unfolded. Now I love
talking to people, making new friends, and
sharing my faith.

I had been a writer for years, but had
never sold a novel. During this healing time,
my books began to be published. My first
novel, *Megan's Choice,* was a reader's favorite, and I was a favorite new author with
Heartsong Presents. *Fireside Christmas*
received four stars from *Romantic Times* and
appeared on the CBA best-seller list for
three months. Then my historical mystery,
Reaping the Whirlwind, won the coveted
Christy Award in 2001. My last release,
Colorado, has sold more than 167,000 copies to date. To God be the glory. Great
things He hath done.

Because I spent so many years struggling
as a beginning writer, I have a heart to help
people who have plenty of talent but who
need personal guidance to cross the hurdle

into publishing. In 2006 I founded ChristianFictionMentors.com, a twelve-lesson interactive program that guides new writers through their first novel.

My husband, David, and I were missionaries on the tiny island of Grenada, West Indies, from 1987 to 2001 with our seven children. While there, I wrote *Survival Cookbook: For Americans Abroad,* 250 recipes for cooking-challenged Americans who can no longer purchase convenience foods. The cookbook is now in its third printing.

I never dreamed that one day I'd love speaking and even appear on radio and television. God continues to broaden my horizons, and I can't thank Him enough.

Visit www.askroseydow.com to ask me any question you may have regarding the writing life, any future books on my horizon, from-scratch cooking questions, or anything at all. You'll see a date there for my next live interview by teleconference. Or visit my Web site at www.roseydow.com. See you there!